AF422106

Cozy Up
to Christmas

a novel about a holiday,
mistaken identity, a cat, and robbery

by Colin Conway

Cozy Up to Christmas

Cover design by Zach McCain

ISBN: 979-8-9852049-2-6

Original Ink Press,
  an imprint of High Speed Creative, LLC
1521 N. Argonne Road, #C-205
Spokane Valley, WA 99212

For Punkin

You can't fool me.
There ain't no sanity clause!

\-   Chico Marx/*A Night at the Opera*

Chapter 1

"What do you want for Christmas?" Ed Belmont asked.

Calvin stared up with slack-jawed fascination as his eyes continued to widen behind smudged glasses. The boy wore an orange winter coat, blue jeans, and oversized black snow boots. An orange and black knitted cap was pulled down over his ears.

Susan Roskam stood behind a camera-mounted tripod. She was a small, thin woman with short blond hair tucked underneath a set of plush reindeer antlers. Susan wore black slacks, a red shirt, and a black sweater with a green Christmas tree in its middle. Multi-colored lights on the tree blinked on and off.

From behind the camera, Susan raised a thumb into the air then waved. She lifted her head from the viewfinder and smiled broadly. "Got a good one!"

Calvin reached for Ed's beard, but the big man pushed the boy's hand away.

Susan stepped over to a line of eleven parents and fourteen children. They all waited anxiously behind a maroon velvet rope linked together by a series of brass stanchions.

Ed knew there were fourteen children because he took the time to count them. He did that while in prison—knowing how many unpleasant things awaited him. Like counting the number of days left in a stretch or how many inmates hostile toward him were in the yard at one time.

Or like now—Ed always knew precisely how many kids waited in line.

"We Wish You a Merry Christmas" played through speakers high above center court for the fortieth time that day. Shoppers walked by with bags in both hands and paused briefly to check out Ed. Some even waved. Occasionally, he returned the gesture. Citizens liked that kind of thing.

Ed leaned slightly toward the boy. "Well?" he asked softly because Susan had said his gravelly voice might intimidate children.

Calvin's tongue slowly peeked out through parted lips—a reluctant turtle exposing its head to the world. The boy continued to stare with awe.

Ed looked at Calvin's mother. She stood on the other side of the rope. Her hands were clasped, and she grinned expectantly. She danced lightly from one foot to the other. The woman wore an orange winter coat, and blue jeans tucked into oversized black snow boots. Long brown hair fell from the orange and black knitted cap pulled tightly down on her head.

Twins, Ed thought. It wasn't the worst way a parent had dressed their child, but it was definitely odd.

He whispered, "Come on, kid. There are others."

When Calvin failed to respond, Ed jerked his knee slightly. This jostled the boy, and he squeaked. His arms flailed, and he started to fall backward, but Ed had a hand on Calvin's back to stop him. The nearby crowd oohed at the boy's clumsiness then laughed with relief at Ed's saving of him.

Calvin's mother stopped dancing, and she stepped toward the velvet rope. As the cord wrapped around her waist, one of the brass stanchions tilted slightly. The mother leaned forward, and her neck stretched out in hopes of being closer to her son.

Ed eyed the kid. "Anything?" This time his voice wasn't so soft.

The boy blinked twice then bent toward him as if to share a secret. "Are you really Santa?"

"What do you think?"

"Are you?"

Ed groaned and looked around, not making eye contact with anything in particular. This was his life until Christmas Day—an endless list of silly demands and misplaced astonishment.

What was with these parents? Ed wondered. Didn't they teach their children anything useful? Like life is unfair, you don't get what you want, and that there's no such thing as Santa.

He inhaled deeply and returned his attention to Calvin. The kid must have been about three. Ed was in his fourth week of this gig, and he'd gotten pretty good at guessing the ages of children. It was a skill he never wanted nor thought he would need to develop.

This sort of phenomenon—the starstruck adulation—frequently happened with the younger ones. The older ones often got straight to their demands—like little terrorists. Even though he didn't like those children any better, Ed appreciated their directness. It got them off his knee faster and moved the line along quicker. Talking with young children was like talking to deranged kittens—neither held any appeal, and the sooner a person could leave them with their mothers so much the better.

"Are you?" Calvin insisted.

"Yeah, sure, kid. I'm Santa. Why else would I be here?"

Here was the Superior Mall in Utopia, Pennsylvania, a declining shopping center in a declining city. The small mall was filled with primarily regional or local stores now, and Ed had learned that the once-proud town had lost a third of its population over the last fifty years.

Calvin reached up and successfully touched Ed's beard. Ed quickly but gently wrapped his gloved hand around the boy's fingers.

"Don't do that," he growled.

The kid's eyes widened again, but this time it was in response to the stern tone.

Ed forced a smile. "If you pull on Santa's beard, you won't get any presents." It was a stupid thing to say, and Ed hoped no one heard him utter those words.

Now blinking uncontrollably, Calvin whimpered, "Santa?"

Ed rolled his head around his shoulders. "I

already told you I was."

Calvin seemed on the verge of tears. "Santa?"

"C'mon, kid. Knock off the waterworks."

"What's going on?" Calvin's mother called out. The brass stanchions on either side of her wobbled as she pushed deeper into the velvet rope.

The line of waiting parents tightened. So long as it wasn't their child, a crying kid on Santa's lap seemed a spectacle that many enjoyed. Perhaps it was like watching a car collision about to happen. The expectation of something terrible occurring to others held some allure.

Calvin's eyes blinked faster, and Ed had to do something quickly. This wouldn't be the first kid to have cried on his lap, but he'd like to avoid another if possible. Ed was a man of action, so he decided to take some.

He pulled Calvin into him, and the boy grunted with surprise. Wrapping his arm around the boy's shoulders, Ed looked up at the concerned mother and smiled. "He wants a football," he announced loud enough so the assembled crowd could hear. Several of the fathers in the group smiled and nodded in approval.

Ed had invented present requests before. Susan had told him children occasionally froze while on Santa's knee. When he started, she gave him a list of suggestions to encourage a child's imagination. All Ed needed was one request from a kid, and he could move on from them. He didn't know many of the items Susan indicated, such as an Xbox, Baby Shark Alphabet Bus, or a Throw Throw Burrito game, so he often went with generic things like a football.

"Santa?" Calvin muttered.

The boy's mother straightened. "A football?" She shook her head as if she'd just eaten a lemon. "Where in the world would he have gotten that idea?"

"A ball, actually," Ed corrected. He saw the confusion on the mother's face and made the quick modification. Maybe she was one of those kinder and gentler parents that didn't want her kid playing football and instead forced them to muddle through a game of soccer. "He wants a ball."

"Are you sure?" the mother asked. Her face remained pickled.

Calvin reached for the beard again, but Ed pushed the kid's hand away. "Knock it off," he whispered. To the mother, Ed nodded. "That's what he said. A ball."

Susan took a nervous step toward Ed then halted. She glanced toward the mother and said, "I heard it, too," but it wasn't delivered with any conviction.

"A ball?" the mother said. "Calvin never plays with them."

Ed cocked his head. "That's why he wants one."

When Ed set Calvin on the ground, the boy reached for the beard again. Ed pushed the little hand away once more.

The mother walked into the velvet rope, dragging the nearest two stanchions behind her. "But a ball is a patriarchal symbol that encourages aggression."

"A what?" Ed said. Now, his face soured, and he glanced at Susan.

She shrugged and mouthed, "I don't know."

The mother continued. "Sports are the patriarchy's way of controlling society. They want to keep us distracted by outdated gender roles, so we don't realize what's really going on with society."

Ed snorted. "Give it a rest, lady."

"Santa?" the mother said.

"He's a boy. Get him a ball." Ed shoved the kid away.

Calvin stutter-stepped toward Susan until she caught him under his arm pits. She hefted him into the air. "Whoa, big fella!" she said. "How was your time with Santa?"

"I want a ball?" the little boy asked.

"I know!" Susan said. "Isn't that great?"

She carried Calvin to his bewildered mother. The two odd-sized twins stared at Ed for a moment before turning to leave.

Ed rested his elbow on the arm of his throne and leaned heavily on it—a reluctant king surveying the kingdom he wished he had never inherited. Several kids stepped out of the waiting line and excitedly waved at him. If Ed ever cursed, now would seem an appropriate time to do so.

Susan came back with an older girl Ed

guessed to be about five. The kid carried a piece of paper in her right hand.

"Santa," Susan said, "this is Charlotte, and she already knows what she wants for Christmas."

Ed lifted the girl onto his knee. "Okay, kid. What is it—"

"Here's my list," Charlotte interrupted, thrusting the paper toward Ed. On it were several items written in crayon. "My parents won't buy me a cell phone, so you need to get it for me. The elves can do that, right?"

Ed looked toward Susan.

The little girl tugged on the arm of his coat to recall his attention. "And I want some make-up. Mom said no, but that should be easy for the elves since they can make a cell phone."

Susan spun on her heel. "Go get 'em, Santa," she said over her shoulder. To the waiting crowd, she called, "Merry Christmas!"

They responded with an equally cheerful, "Merry Christmas!"

Chapter 2

"I've been a good girl this year," Marjorie Lewis said. Her elbows rested on the round table, and she settled her chin onto the back of her interlaced fingers. Several shiny bracelets on each arm had slid down to gather around her forearms.

When Marjorie sighed, Ed Belmont grunted into the sandwich now stuck in his mouth.

They were sitting in the Superior Mall's breakroom. It was tucked in an out-of-the-way corridor past the restrooms, the maintenance room, and the mall office. The breakroom was for the mall employees, and a small, printed sign on the door even said as much. Shop owners and their staff weren't supposed to be there. Still, with the decline of interest from national retailers, the mall's manager figured one more amenity might be attractive to local business owners. Now, anyone that worked in the mall could use the breakroom.

Marjorie owned Pet Shop Bays, a boutique catering to the beautification of dogs and cats. She was about Ed's age with dark hair and bright eyes—the kind that revealed an out-sized hopefulness in life. She always dressed as if she were stepping out of some 1980s music video—with too much color and too many shiny bracelets.

"Like really good," she said.

"I'm on break, Marjorie."

Ed's beard and hat were stacked on top of his black leather gloves in the chair next to him. The red Santa jacket was draped over the back of his chair. He could have put these articles of clothing in the nearby bank of small lockers that were set aside for employees, but they were useful as a buffer between him and the overeager Marjorie. His biceps bulged against the white cotton t-shirt, and the tattoos on his arms and right hand were now exposed.

Marjorie craned her head slightly forward. "But you never let me tell you what I want for Christmas."

His lip curled. "I don't want to know."

"Come on, let me sit on your lap."

"No."

"But you're Santa."

"You're too old for Santa." He bit into his sandwich.

"No one is ever too old for Santa. What is that? A PB&J?"

It was. He'd eaten the same lunch for the past four weeks. There wasn't anything wrong with peanut butter and jelly sandwiches. They were something he could easily make, then store while working. He'd also brought along a banana and a bag of peanuts.

Marjorie flicked her fingers toward his lunch. "I can make you something better. Be happy to if you let me."

"No," Ed said through a mouthful. "Go away."

He would have been politer, but this scene had played out in some fashion for the past three weeks, ever since Marjorie had stumbled upon him in the breakroom. Her store had a line-of-sight on the Santa set, so now whenever Ed took his breaks, Marjorie closed her shop and showed up here. So far, his rudeness had failed to deter her advances.

"What do you do after you leave the mall?"

Case in point, Ed thought. He shoved the last of his sandwich into his mouth.

"You never tell me. I bet you don't eat so good at home either. Why don't you let me fix you up something nice?" She reached out for him, but he was a little too far away. Ed congratulated himself on the idea of placing his uniform in the nearby chair. The first time Marjorie found him in the breakroom, she sat next to him, forcing him to end his lunch quickly. "We could show each other our tattoos. I have a tattoo, too." She giggled. "I bet you didn't know about my tattoo."

Susan Roskam entered the breakroom then. "Ed doesn't want to know about your tattoo, Marge. Leave the man alone."

The store owner looked up. "Don't call me that. You know I hate it. Besides, what's it to you, Suzy? I'm not bothering him." Marjorie looked earnestly at Ed. "Am I bothering you?"

"Yeah," he said, "you are."

Marjorie giggled again. "You're so funny." She reached out to touch him but missed by several inches. "I love your sense of humor."

Susan picked up Ed's hat, beard, and gloves

and set them on the table. Marjorie tried to move into the now empty seat, but Susan sat first and blocked her. "It's time for you to go. I need to talk business with Ed."

Marjorie pouted. "I can sit here quietly."

Susan leaned toward her. "I said go, Marge, or I'll tell Ed about that time you went out with—"

The store owner popped up so quickly it sent her chair skittering backward. "I'm leaving."

"That's right," Susan said, "you're leaving."

"You don't have to be so mean."

"I'm not the one who—"

"I said I was leaving!" Marjorie turned to Ed and playfully waved. "I'll see you later." After a final glare at Susan, she hurried from the room.

Ed asked, "What were you threatening Marjorie with?"

"Small town gossip," Susan said. "Never mind about that. We've got a problem. Two problems, actually."

Ed peeled his banana. "I'm Santa. My day is nothing but problems."

"Stop bellyaching. I'm serious." The plush reindeer ears and the blinking sweater argued differently.

"What's the first problem?" Ed asked.

"That deranged Santa struck again. You know the one?"

Ed had heard talk of it.

"He just robbed the liquor store over on Third Street, near the edge of town."

"How's that a problem for us?"

Susan appeared offended. "It's bad for the brand. There is some maniac out there besmirching the good name of Santa. That's going to depress turnout."

"Seems to me we've been doing fine."

She dismissively waved her hand. "We could be doing better. I compared our numbers against last year, and we're down."

"Maybe you had a better Santa."

She scoffed. "Uh, no. Chet was a loon. I mean, he did all right with the kids, but he gave me nothing but trouble. Always taking time off, showing up late, lying about stuff, getting into arguments with parents. It never ended."

"And that's why I'm here. Do you think this Chet guy could be robbing the convenience stores?"

Susan shook her head. "No."

"Then there's nothing we can do about it." Ed pulled the banana from its peel. "What's the second problem?"

"We need to make an appearance for the fundraiser."

He eyed her. "We?"

"Okay, you. Santa."

Ed pointed the banana at himself. "Why me?"

Susan flopped back into her chair. "Because it's in my contract with the mall—there shall be no other Santa before me. Or you, in this case. And the fundraiser wanted to bring in their own Santa. Imagine what would happen if there were two Santas in the mall at the same time."

Ed tossed the peel into the trash can.

"Imagine."

"It's a space-time continuum thing." Susan clapped her hands together and quickly parted them. "Boom. The entire kid world would implode. Or is it explode? Yeah, definitely explode. That's why I have a rider in the contract to avoid a moment like that. So, the fundraiser isn't happy, and that's why we—*you*—have to make an appearance."

"Why are they holding the fundraiser here and now?"

"It's not here and now. They've been raising funds for the whole year. Every shop has had those big water jug-type jars in their stores. You know what I'm talking about?"

He did. He'd seen the jugs near the cash registers in most of the stores.

Susan continued. "And Hurley is part of the fundraising team. He thinks the extra holiday shoppers will bring one final push to the effort."

John Hurley was the mall manager and a guy that Ed hadn't gotten along with since his first day. Some things don't mix well—fire and ice, oil and water, Hurley and Belmont.

Ed bit his banana. Through a mouthful, he asked, "Am I getting paid extra?"

"Santa isn't greedy."

He grimaced. "I'm not Santa."

"It's during your workday."

"In that case, it sounds fun." It didn't, and his tone reflected as much.

Susan leaned forward. "Going to the fundraiser means you don't have to have a kid on your lap."

Ed cocked his head.

"See? There's a silver lining to everything."

"When are we doing this thing?"

"In a couple hours." Susan motioned toward Ed's half-eaten banana. "Now, hurry up and finish your lunch. There's a line out there, and a bunch of kids are waiting to see you." She poked him in the arm.

"They don't want to see me. They want to see the suit."

"You're such a grumpy Gus. How can you not be in the holiday spirit? It's the happiest time of the year!" She touched the edge of her sweater, and "Jingle Bells" erupted from a speaker hidden somewhere within. "Don't you just love this holiday?"

Ed bit the banana again and grumbled, "Merry Christmas."

Chapter 3

"Merry Christmas," US Marshal Gayle Goodspeed said as she loudly plopped a manila envelope onto the table.

Beauregard Smith paused before he slid into the booth. "It's not even Thanksgiving."

"Almost, so consider it an early present." Goodspeed dropped into her seat and reached for a menu. "What do you think is good here? I could eat a horse."

They were at Teddy's Burgers in Toledo, Ohio. The restaurant was packed with a late-lunch crowd. Light rock & roll played over the noise of customers dining.

Nearby, a harried mother wrangled three noisy boys as they waited for their food to arrive.

Beau dropped into the booth, opened the envelope, and pulled a thin file from it. A thought occurred to him. "When did you pick this up?"

"Got it from a guy when we walked in. Hey, they got a tenderloin sandwich here. Ever have one of those? They're delicious."

He looked around. Somehow, he missed the handoff. Beau led the way into the restaurant, and Goodspeed had followed. He hadn't noticed a guy carrying an envelope.

The marshal continued. "Check out the triple cheeseburger. Maybe you should try that. With all the driving I've done, I could probably eat two horses." She looked up. "Why do people always want to eat horses when they're hungry? What did a horse ever do to us? Wouldn't it be better if we said I'm so hungry I could eat a politician?"

Beau stared at the marshal. His fingers held the edge of the folder, ready to flip it open. Goodspeed was in a cheerful mood, and that worried him. She was ordinarily cranky, or at least slightly irritable. But now she was being downright nice, and that was suspicious.

She was his witness inspector, and her job was to protect him. Goodspeed didn't inspire the confidence that his first witness inspector had, but so far, the frail, older woman had managed to keep him safe. Although, she played the game a bit differently than his first inspector had.

Beau released the file's edge and put his hand on it. "What's wrong with this?"

From behind her menu, Goodspeed said, "What do you mean what's wrong with it?" Now, her head popped into view. "Nothing's wrong with it, you big sissy. That may be my best work ever, and I'm talking my whole career, thank you very much."

Beau stabbed the file with a single finger. "The last place was supposed to be good, too."

"It was good." The marshal returned to studying her menu. "And I didn't mess that up, by the way. You did."

"The cover you gave me—"

Goodspeed clucked. "Was fine. There was nothing wrong with it."

"You named me after a woman."

The marshal looked over the top of her menu again. "Skeeter Dursky was a darned fine singer. You should be so lucky."

"Should be? I *was* Skeeter Dursky."

"You complain a lot."

Beau stabbed the file again. "Am I going to hate the name?"

"The name is fine. It's a good name." She nodded absently as she read the menu. The marshal looked up when she realized Beau was still staring at her. "Dear Lord in heaven. Trust me. You'll like it."

"What about the job?"

"It's temporary."

Beau cocked his head. "What's that mean?"

Her gaze returned to the menu. "It means what it means. We'll move you when the season is over."

"I have to move again even though nothing bad has happened?"

"Are you going to order?" Goodspeed released her menu, and it flopped to the table. "I'm not the one who created this mess. I'm just the one trying to clean it up."

Beau met her glare. She was right. Goodspeed hadn't created the situation he was in—he had. He'd gotten involved with the Satan's Dawgs, an outlaw motorcycle club based in Phoenix, Arizona. At first, the club was everything he needed—a safe place, a home, a family. But after a time, it was perverted into a money-making machine that loaned out his skills as bookkeeper to the highest bidder.

The Dawgs disguised their most essential functions with coded names. His job was to run a tally of those who had crossed the club—*keep the books* in club parlance. Now and then, he settled those scores—or cleared the books. Beau Smith was good at his job, and there was a line of dead men to prove it. The cops and the feds had never found any of them.

But an enterprising FBI agent wanted to break the club, and he discovered the one thing that Beau loved—his grandmother. It was the weakness that turned him from a feared killer into the thing he dreaded most in the world—a rat.

"If you don't pick something to eat, I'll pick it for you." The marshal lifted her menu. "And if you're so worried about the job, open it, and you'll see."

Beau pushed the folder away. "No."

Goodspeed motioned toward the file. "Stop being a baby and open it."

A server approached and delivered plates to the mother and three young boys at the nearby table. When she finished setting down the meals, the woman turned to Beau and Goodspeed. She was a young woman with a genial smile. "Can I bring you folks something to get started with? Iced tea or a soda?"

"Just a couple of waters," the marshal said. "My friend hasn't decided on what to order yet. He's a sensitive eater."

The server placed her hand on the edge of the

table. "Oh, I totally understand. My father has the same thing. We've got some vegan options that might work for you. Maybe that would be gentler on your stomach."

"Oh, vegan," Goodspeed said to Beau. "How does that sound?"

"No."

The server smiled politely. "I'll give you a few more minutes."

When she left, Goodspeed's face hardened. "Open the folder."

Beau crossed his arms. "It's going to be bad. I know it."

"Do it now, Little Sister."

The marshal was grouchy again and calling him names. This was the Gayle Goodspeed Beau knew. The two were on familiar footing again. He was a little relieved. The happy law enforcement officer creeped him out.

"Whatever." Beau flipped open the file and leaned over it. "Ed Belmont," he muttered then glanced up. "Not bad. It's decent. Better than Skeeter."

"I disagree," Goodspeed said, "but you're welcome to your opinion."

"Belmont sounds like an insurance salesman's name. It's something to work with, though. Ed Belmont." He repeated the last name a few times. "Hi, I'm Ed Belmont. Hey, what the heck is this? Says here he grew up in Minnesota." Beau turned his palms upward in a what-were-you-thinking gesture. "You know how I feel about Minnesota."

The marshal chuckled. "Then you won't forget where you grew up."

Beau's lip curled. "But Minnesota? You might as well have said I grew up in Canada."

Goodspeed's face flattened. "Even I have limits, Beau."

He grunted and returned his attention to Ed Belmont's fact sheet. No criminal history, so he wouldn't have to memorize anything there. No college. No military service. He flipped to the next page.

"Where's Utopia?"

Goodspeed's gaze softened and took on a faraway look. "That's what we all want to know."

Beau's finger stabbed the page. "Says here I'll be living in Utopia, Pennsylvania."

"An oxymoron," the marshal said. "It's in the western part of the state, just north of Pittsburgh. On the Ohio border, right across from Youngstown. Still not ringing a bell?"

Beau shook his head.

"Well, there you will be."

He bowed his head over the file again. "Also says I'm working for Holiday Delivery Systems, LLC? What is that? Am I carrying packages or something?"

Goodspeed smiled once more. Man, he distrusted that grin.

"Merry Christmas," she said.

"I don't get it."

"It's ingenious really." Goodspeed put her menu to the side. "It's a place where you can hide in the open while wearing a mask and gloves. Why I never thought of it before to hide that stupid tattoo is beyond me." She pointed at the inky ball of fire on the back of his right hand. The rest of the tattoos on his arms were hidden under his jacket.

Beau rubbed the ball of fire. "There's nothing wrong with this tattoo."

"Except every mobster in the world knows what to look for."

She was referring to the mob's website—thefbiisabunchofdirtyrats.com—the repository for everyone the mob knew to be in the witness protection program. Beau discovered this website through his previous witness inspector and even saw his own picture on it. The Satan's Dawgs had somehow linked with the mob to help spread the word of his betrayal to the rest of the underworld.

Then Beau made the mistake of crossing the mob in the first town he was hidden in. He killed one of their east coast leaders. He'd done so to protect Daphne Winterbourne—a woman he'd met and fallen for. In fact, he still pined for her.

The marshal said, "We should get that thing removed. They can do that now. Laser surgery or something."

"Fine," Beau said. "You pay for it."

"No kidding, we'll pay for it. Like you're going to pay for it."

He bent over the file again. "Back to this job thing. I don't get it. I've got to wear a uniform while I deliver packages? Am I like a UPS driver or something?"

"Something like that. Say ho-ho-ho."

Beau scrunched his nose. "Ho-ho-ho?"

The marshal laughed. "You're going to do great. Now, let's order."

He really hated that she was in a good mood. Beau lowered his gaze to study the folder again, but almost immediately, his head popped up. "You're kidding."

"No, I'm hungry. Maybe I'll have the Humpty Dumpty. It's got an egg on it."

Beau slammed the file shut. "I can't do this job. I don't like kids. I might even hate them."

He glanced to the nearby table to watch the mother with her three boys. The kids had ketchup and mustard on their faces and were loudly laughing. One boy had two French fries stuck in his nose. Another had two straws dangling similarly. The third was now trying to stick a couple of spoon handles up his. The mother hung her head in a defeated fashion.

Beau's gaze returned to the marshal. "I stand corrected. I definitely hate them."

"That's perfect," Goodspeed said. "Stick with that. People can trust you with their kids if you have that kind of attitude."

"Because I hate them?"

"Better than a big, tattooed man saying he loves children. That would give most normal folks the willies." She shivered. "Gross."

Beau tapped his chest. "But I'm not old."

"You don't have to be old to be Santa. They got wigs and fake beards for that."

"But I'm not fat."

"Which is why I suggested the triple cheeseburger."

"I'm not eating that, and I'm not doing this."

Goodspeed smiled. "It's already done. You're jolly ol' Saint Nick, or you're in the cold all by your lonesome. It's your choice."

Beau grunted. "Those are terrible choices."

"Such is life."

"Why aren't you putting me into another business owned by the marshal service?"

Beau's previous witness inspector had settled him into two enterprises owned by the marshals. That allowed him a fair amount of autonomy. At his last location, Goodspeed procured him a job as a maintenance man for a retirement community. He was on the bottom rung and responsible for all the grunt work.

"Just how many businesses do you think we own?"

Beau shrugged.

"Not enough," the marshal said. "And you burned two of them in a matter of weeks. We'll never get them back. Those types of gigs are great assignments. Wonderful, in fact. We've had people spend their entire protection periods in one of our businesses."

"I'll do better," Beau said. "I promise. Anything but this."

"After what you've pulled, I'd get myself canned if I assigned you another of our businesses."

"I haven't pulled anything. None of it was my fault."

"Keep telling yourself that, Little Sister." The marshal picked up Beau's menu and put it on top of the Ed Belmont file. "Now, hurry up and pick something. The waitress is coming back, and I'm ready to eat that politician."

Chapter 4

Ed Belmont stood at the edge of the small platform and waved to the gathered crowd. It was a large assembly, possibly several hundred people. It may have been the most shoppers Ed had seen in the mall since his arrival in Utopia.

Most of the crowd waved back, and several even cheered. It was a surreal experience to Ed since he knew they weren't waving or hollering for him—they were doing so for Santa.

Overhead, "A Holly Jolly Christmas" played throughout the mall.

On his left were several members of the fundraising committee. They all wore nice-fitting suits. Among them was the mall manager, John Hurley, who was dressed in black pants, black shoes, and a long-sleeved plaid shirt. The man tended to wear the same black pants and shoes every day—only the shirt changed.

To Ed's right stood a waving Susan Roskam. She still wore the plush reindeer antlers. The lights in her sweater blinked a new, nauseatingly cheerful pattern. "We're going to get a big line after this," she whispered from the side of her mouth. "Look at all those kids out there. Cha-ching." She elbowed him. "Say it."

"Cha-ching."

Susan turned to him with a stern look. "Give

the people what they want."

Ed frowned, but she wasn't deterred. She probably couldn't see the look of displeasure hidden under the silly beard.

Susan's face brightened as she faced the crowd. She waved at them again, but only a handful responded accordingly. They seemed to be waiting for Ed—*for Santa*—to do something.

A thought occurred to Ed then. An unhappy thought. He was a man pretending to be someone pretending to be someone else.

"Now," Susan whispered, then fervently waved some more.

No hands in the crowd responded to her, but there were some grumblings. The crowd was growing restless.

"I'm not a performing monkey," Ed muttered.

Susan elbowed him in the ribs—harder this time.

There was no bothering to fight it any further. This was Ed's lot in life. For now, he was a performing monkey. Due to his bad choices in life, the government had made him one. This was the price for freedom. Ed inhaled deeply, then called out, "Ho-ho-ho!"

The crowd cheered, and several kids gleefully squealed.

Susan clapped her hands and looked toward the center of the stage.

From behind a podium, John Hurley watched Ed and Susan with open contempt. The mall manager was a short, bald man. His disdain quickly vanished into a practiced smile before he turned toward the crowd. Stepping up to the microphone, he said, "Thanks for coming, Santa! Is there something you want to say to all the parents?"

Ed shook his head.

Hurley's brow furrowed, and he looked toward Susan.

She leaned into Ed's ear. "Tell them to give more."

He grunted, "No."

"Do it."

"I'm not a salesman."

"You're Santa. This is what Santa does."

"Santa is a fundraising shill?"

Susan shoved him in the back and said, "Go."

Ed stumbled to the podium. This bumbling walk elicited giggles from some nearby children.

Behind the podium and the assembled fundraising committee stood a giant billboard that read *Fundraiser for the Utopian Village—a Playground Paradise*. There was also a large pyramid of clear plastic water jugs filled with coins and dollars bills.

Along with the Parks Department, this local committee wanted to raise money to purchase a piece of downtown land to build a playground. In the crowd were the mayor, two city council members, and the former star of a short-run children's TV show who had returned to Utopia to live a quiet life away from Hollywood.

Ed as Santa was the final speaker for the event. He stepped up to the microphone and cleared his throat. Because of his proximity to the microphone, it echoed throughout the mall.

At the edge of the crowd, Marjorie Lewis smiled brightly and waved. She cupped a small Chihuahua in her left arm.

Ed bent toward the microphone. "Hey—" Feedback screeched through the speakers. Ed straightened and backed away from the microphone. He waited for a moment before trying again. "You all know me. I'm Santa."

Several children cheered, "Santa!" at the same time.

However, Marjorie's call for "Santa!" came out late and became a one-woman celebration of Ed. Several adults in the crowd turned disapprovingly toward her. Marjorie didn't seem embarrassed by her outburst.

Ed cleared his throat again. He wasn't used to standing in front of a crowd this large, and the throat clearing seemed to be a nervous response. It rattled loudly through the speakers. "Anyway," he said. "All you parents, make sure you give more to the park." Ed glanced to Susan. She was rolling her hand in a motion for him to continue. He turned back to the microphone. "It'll be good for the kids and stuff."

With a single nod of satisfaction, Ed stepped away from the podium.

The crowd politely clapped, and once again Marjorie cheered, "Santa!" She lifted the little dog into the air and shook its paw in a hello manner.

John Hurley approached the podium. Without any enthusiasm, he said, "That was

Santa, folks."

Susan's face contorted as Ed headed toward her.

The mall manager continued to speak but now took on a salesman's enthusiasm. "Break out those wallets. Let's finish this year with a big contribution. I know it's Christmas, but let's do something that will last long-term for the children and the community!"

When the crowd moved to disperse, Ed and Susan descended from the stage. The mall manager hurried over and looked down at Ed. "What the heck was that?"

"What are you talking about?"

Hurley threw his arms into the air. "'It'll be good for the kids and *stuff?*' Talk about phoning it in."

Ed scowled. "Back off, man. I'm Santa—not some hack for your cause."

The manager's face reddened, and he pointed at Ed. "You're whatever I need you to be."

"I don't work for you."

Hurley motioned toward Susan. "You work for her. And she's a vendor in this mall. The mall that I'm the manager of." He straightened and put his hands on his hips. "Consider me the lord of this manor. The ruler of this kingdom."

Susan chuckled.

Hurley sneered at her. "Careful, Missy. You're lucky you're in center court. What if I moved you to the far end of the mall next year? Would you like that?"

Susan raised her hands in a calming fashion.

"Easy, John. There's no need to be that way. You and I both know Santa works best in center court."

"A good Santa, maybe, but this guy?" He thumbed toward Ed. "Chet was better than this bump, and he was a nut job."

Ed stared at the manager.

"You think that evil eye intimidates me? I'm the one who does the intimidating around here," Hurley pointed at Ed. "Don't you ever forget that."

Ed wouldn't. When he was the bookkeeper for the Satan's Dawgs, this was the type of thing that might make it into the club's accounting. Oh, it wouldn't require Ed to do something as drastic as dragging the man into a field and leaving him there permanently. But pulling a guy into an alley for some knuckle counseling was always good for an attitude adjustment. John Hurley seemed a candidate ripe for that type of thing.

But Ed couldn't do that anymore. Not only was he on the run and hiding in the Witness Protection Program, but he was also Santa. Jolly old St. Nick was not allowed to assault other people. It just wasn't done.

Hurley spun on his heel and walked away.

Susan grabbed Ed's arm. "Let's take a stroll. Burn off this conversation and maybe drum up some extra business before we go back."

As they walked through the mall, Susan smiled brightly and waved at everyone she met. Ed shuffled along and half-heartedly waggled his hand whenever someone called out, "Santa!"

Susan detoured those parents who tried to get an impromptu picture of their children with Ed. Much to the dismay of those folks hoping to save on the cost of an annual picture, Susan stopped them with a gleeful, "We'll be back at center court in fifteen minutes."

They walked by various businesses—none of which Ed had heard of before. Nails So U, Hair Today—Gone Tomorrow, and Kitchen Stitches. There were even non-retail tenants like a small church, a candidate for governor's headquarters, and a local real estate office. There were many vacant suites.

Security Officer Eileen Webster leaned against the entry to one of the empty spaces and watched Ed and Susan approach. She was a taller woman and about the same age as Ed and Susan. Even though there was no gun, the duty belt Eileen wore around her thin waist looked heavy as it was loaded with gadgets—handcuffs, pepper spray, flashlight, baton, keys, and cell phone.

"Hey, Ed."

Susan hissed, "It's Santa." She glanced around before saying, "He's *Santa*."

Ed nodded toward the security officer. "Afternoon, Eileen."

Being friendly to cops and security guards wasn't part of Ed's makeup in his previous life. However, since the radical change in his life, he'd had a couple of experiences where being nice to the law and its related entities had worked out for him.

"Where'd you park your reindeer?" Eileen asked with a smile.

Susan looked around. "Be quiet, Lee. Some kids might hear you."

Eileen pushed off the entryway and stepped over to them. "Suzy, you need to get over yourself and relax. It's only Christmas."

Susan inhaled sharply, then clamped her mouth shut. Her bloated cheeks reddened as her sweater continued to blink its crazy rhythm. She angrily shook her head, which twisted the plush antlers.

Eileen tugged on the sleeve of Ed's jacket. "What's with all the hoopla anyway? Christmas comes around every year. People don't get this excited for Arbor Day, and that's a holiday that actually does some good."

Susan's eyes narrowed. "There's something wrong with you."

"You should be careful, Ed. Some clown dressed like you is running around town holding up liquor stores."

"I heard," he said.

Eileen pulled once more on the sleeve of his jacket before letting go. "I don't want you being confused for him. Seeing as how you're so important to Christmas and all."

Susan jerked Ed's arm. "Let's go. We've got kids waiting."

Eileen said, "You should be careful, too, Suzy."

She stopped. "Why? What did I do?"

"You know who is back."

Susan's face hardened. "Chet? What's he doing here?"

"He said he wanted to do some shopping. I told him to steer clear of you."

Ed glanced between the two women. "That's the guy I replaced, right?"

Eileen nodded. "He's a piece of work. Good with the kids, but about as friendly as a cornered wolverine to anyone else. Seems he's pretty upset that he didn't get to be Santa this year."

Susan glanced at Ed. "Don't let it bother you."

He smiled. "Why would I be bothered?" Ed had faced tougher guys than an upset former mall Santa.

Susan jerked her head. "We've got to get back." She didn't sound as enthusiastic as before.

Eileen pointed at Ed. "Remember what I said. Be careful out there. I don't want you getting confused with some two-bit robber."

Chapter 5

Ed walked back toward his apartment. He wore a leather jacket, jeans, and black boots. A stocking cap was pulled down over his ears, and his hands were shoved into his pockets. It was cold but not snowing. A couple of times earlier in the week, it had already done that, and a thin layer of snow remained on the ground.

He didn't own a car, but that wasn't necessary for his current life in Utopia. Anywhere he couldn't walk, he could catch a bus.

The stroll felt good because it reminded him of freedom. It wasn't as symbolic as riding his motorcycle, but he couldn't do that for obvious reasons beyond the weather. He'd hidden it in a storage unit in Wyoming until someday when the heat from all this recent activity died down. Then he'd go and collect it.

But he couldn't truly be free as long as the government had him in the Witness Protection Program. However, it was better than the alternative—at least, for the moment.

There was a woman in Maine that he wanted to get back to see once more. The desire to be near Daphne Winterbourne was growing stronger the longer he was apart from her. That was an odd feeling for Ed. He wasn't used to yearning for a woman. He'd never done such a thing.

Was he deifying Daphne in some way? Building her up to be more than she was?

He'd only gotten to know her for a short time. Maybe the weeks since he had left Maine so abruptly were playing tricks on his mind. Perhaps he didn't truly miss her but rather the idea of what they might have been together.

No, Ed thought. Daphne Winterbourne was special. It *was* as simple as that.

He detoured from his path and headed toward the Quik N Go, a convenience store with so many advertisements plastered in its various windows that it was impossible to see inside.

The doorbell dinged as he entered, and a country-rap song played on the radio.

Behind the counter stood a mid-twenties white man. A camouflaged baseball hat sat catawampus on his head. The clerk sang along with the tune playing throughout the store, and he mimed several dance moves. "Running through the fields with the early morning dew/gotta keep my boys moving with the harvest crews."

When he noticed Ed, the clerk stopped singing and asked, "What up, yo?"

"Just need a few things."

"That's good. That's good." He flicked his hand. "Help yourself. Do your thing." The clerk returned to mumbling the lyrics and pantomiming his vision of country-rap stardom.

Ed grabbed a Big Time frozen burrito and a bag of jalapeno chips. He set the items down on the counter. The clerk stopped dancing and moved toward the cash register. The name tag attached to his Grand Theft Auto t-shirt read *Nathan*.

"Going for the Big Time," Nathan said. *"El grande burrito."* His Spanish was mangled and exaggerated—probably like most of Nathan's educational career.

Posted on a Plexiglas shield next to the cash register was a *Have You Seen?* flyer from the police department. It featured a photograph of Santa Claus pointing a gun at another clerk from a different store. Ed leaned in to get a better look. The Santa garb fit the suspect perfectly. He made a good-looking Father Christmas.

"Yo, man, you got nothing to be worried about."

Ed straightened. "Yeah?"

"For real. If that fool decides to come here—" Nathan stuck two fingers out and pulled his thumb back in the universal symbol for a gun. He then turned it sideways and lifted it to eye level. "Clack, clack. Down goes ol' Saint Nick." Nathan smacked his chest with both hands. "After that, I'm a hero with keys to a Bentley. A small-town boy made good."

"You've got a gun?"

Nathan reached behind his back but didn't pull it out. "Never ask a man if he's strapped. That's a good way to get yourself got."

Ed raised his eyebrows. "Ever fire that gun?"

The clerk brought his empty hand forward.

"Yo, I've been in war zones all around the world, G. Even got the rewards to prove it."

"You mean awards?"

Nathan waved his hands in front of him. "Rewards, awards, they're all the same. Listen, I've been training for years. *Call of Duty. Fortnite. Gears of War.*" He ticked them off on his fingers. "Don't forget *Apex Legends.*"

"Video games?"

"Don't say it like that, man. Those games are *tactical simulations*, yo. The same as going to war, but smarter." Nathan tapped the side of his skull. "I'm a straight killer and didn't have to risk an ounce of my blood for the training." He snapped his fingers. "That's for real."

"Impressive."

"That's what I'm saying." Nathan turned to the cash register and announced a total. "All I gotta say is that red-suited fool best watch hisself. 'Silent Night' is gonna have a whole new meaning if he comes in here."

The clerk slipped the items into a bag and took Ed's money.

"Sounds like you've got it all figured out."

Nathan sucked air through his front teeth. "Play the game, or it plays you. Them's the rules."

Ed took the bag and headed toward the exit. Before he stepped outside, Ed looked back. Nathan was already rhyming along with the next country-rap song on the radio.

*****

When Ed opened the door to his second-floor apartment, a cat darted across the apartment. It disappeared behind the couch.

"Travis," Ed said. "Good to see you, too."

Scattered about were the tell-tale signs of the tom's rampage through the apartment. A coffee cup lay on the kitchen floor with its now broken handle several inches away. A small trash can was on its side—most of its contents were spilled out. A skein of yarn was pulled out and run about the apartment. A paperback novel was also on the floor.

For a moment, Ed ignored the detritus and entered the kitchen. The floors creaked as he moved about. After slipping the Big Time burrito from its wrapper, Ed started the microwave. Then he cleaned up the waste basket.

"Aren't dogs supposed to do this type of thing?"

Travis came out from his hiding space to rub on Ed's leg. He pushed the tom away. "Remember our deal."

Ed picked up the coffee cup that featured a logo from a local bank. It was with the apartment when he moved in. He tossed the broken handle into the trash bin. The cup would work fine without it.

Next, he collected the knitting needles and re-wrapped the skein of yarn. He had learned how to knit from his grandmother and did it as a way to calm his nerves. Ed never knitted anything to completion—he simply knitted for a while then undid the rows of stitches before putting the yarn and needles away.

He often knitted after clearing the books for the club. A lot of the other Dawgs self-medicated when they finished with particularly stressful jobs. Most of them thought knitting was a strange habit, but no one argued with Ed's effectiveness—the effectiveness of his former self, he corrected.

Finally, Ed retrieved the paperback—Richard Stark's *The Hunter*. He'd never been much of a reader—only repair manuals and the occasional newspaper—until he met Daphne Winterbourne. She thought he was the owner of a mystery bookstore and went on about how much she read. To impress her, Ed lied about his reading. Then he actually read a book. Then a second.

Now, he lived above a used bookstore. Ed didn't have a TV, so every night he spent time reading. When he finished *The Hunter* it would be the fourth book since he'd moved to Utopia— one a week. He was getting to be a fast reader. That made him feel proud.

He wanted to call Daphne and talk with her about the books he'd read so far. Except for the current novel, the others had all been Travis McGee novels, which he knew Daphne liked. He wondered if she'd ever read *The Hunter*, but he couldn't ask her because doing so would violate the simple rules that the marshal service gave him.

Do not contact people from your old life.

Do not visit places from your old life.
Do not develop habits from your old life.

Ed initially thought the rules were only there to protect him. He didn't realize how important they were to others until he bought some postcards in Oregon. It was supposed to be a simple act—something to send Daphne so she would know he was thinking about her.

Unfortunately, the Dawgs tracked him to that coastal town and found the postcards he'd written and addressed. He'd left them in his hotel room. To protect Daphne, Ed killed a man to recover those cards.

Now, Ed couldn't risk writing any letters or even calling Daphne from the burner phone he had hidden underneath his pillow. The best he could do was remember her. That would have to suffice. He wanted to imagine them reconnecting somewhere under better circumstances, but that was a childish dream, and Ed didn't go for that sort of thing.

The microwave dinged.

Before sitting to eat and read, Ed refilled the cat's food and water bowls.

For now, he was eager to get back to his book. He wanted to know what was going on in the world of Parker—a career criminal. That was a man he understood.

Chapter 6

As soon as he entered the mall, they came at Ed—twenty of them with their arms swinging and legs churning. The group took the entire width of the hallway. Even though there was still an hour to go before the mall officially opened for business, the gray-haired mass prowled the corridor like they owned the joint.

Ed stepped out of the way, and the mall walkers hurried by. He pulled back the brown paper sack holding his lunch to avoid being struck by an errant hand.

Two of the older women waved at Ed. He smiled and returned the gesture. Citizens expected that type of behavior, and it was best he blended in. Besides, he liked being liked. That was different than his days with the Satan's Dawgs. Back then, he wanted to be feared. It seemed the better way to live. He was wrong.

Even though the mall hadn't officially opened yet, "Jingle Bell Rock" played through its speakers. Ed had heard the song at least six times a day—maybe even twice that amount— since he'd started working as Santa. The Christmas music was on a loop, and he knew the next song in the rotation was "Silver Bells."

An older man Ed knew as Arlo brought up the rear. He wore a dirty *US Air Force* hat with a curled brim, a t-shirt that read *Proud Veteran*, and blue sweatpants with *Nittnay Lions* emblazoned on the left leg. Arlo stopped and bent at the waist. He lifted a hand for Ed to wait, then took a deep, raspy breath.

"The pace got you today?" Ed asked.

Arlo straightened. "Got me nothing. I've been at this for an hour now. What have you done with your morning?"

Actually, Ed woke up and finished reading his book. He was quite proud of that accomplishment as it had only taken him four days. That was a personal best. Now, he needed a new book. The possibility of what to read next excited him, and he felt slightly nerdy for it. Was this how Daphne felt after finishing a book?

"Well?" the older man asked. "What were you doing? Probably lollygagging around with some filly. I remember those days." His brow furrowed. "Sort of."

Ed eyed the group of mall walkers getting further away. With the hand holding his lunch sack, he pointed down the hall. "Shouldn't you hurry along? They're getting away."

The older man shooed them off. "They'll come back. It's a loop. That's how this works. I hear the pet store lady's got big eyes for you." Arlo wiggled his eyebrows. "Was she the one that slowed your morning?"

"No."

Arlo nodded. "Good man. That's a solid policy—never kiss and tell. Speaking of which, did the cops talk to you yet?"

"What for?"

The older man stepped back. "What do you mean what for? Don't you watch the news?"

"I don't have a TV."

"What century are you living in? Watch it on your phone, boy. Don't you got one?"

He did, but his phone wasn't smart—it only made and received calls. And he only had it in case of an emergency. He never carried it around. That was so he wouldn't be tempted to make a call to Daphne Winterbourne or his grandmother. If he had to find the phone to use it, he'd be less likely to do something rash.

"Arlo, why do the cops want to talk with me?"

The older man's eyes narrowed. "Santa beat up the mall manager last night."

"Wasn't me."

"I know it wasn't you. I said it was Santa, but it ain't no secret you and that manager are cross ways." Arlo bumped his fists against one another.

"I don't have a problem with Hurley."

"That almost sounded convincing." Arlo chuckled. "Stick to that when the cops come around."

"I'm going to."

"All you Santa's look alike, I suppose." Arlo glanced down the hall in the direction the mall walkers had departed. His neck craned forward, and his eyes narrowed. "Ah, heck. I think they're coming back. Is that them?"

"It's them. Listen, did Hurley say it was me?"

The older man's gaze returned to Ed. "I don't

know, but it's obvious he don't like you. I've seen it with my own two eyes, and I don't see too good. What did you do to him?"

"Nothing. I never did anything to him."

Arlo reached out for Ed. "Hey, if my wife asks, tell her you stopped me. She gives me an earful when I take these breaks."

"In that case," Ed said, "you're on your own. I don't need to get in the middle of a domestic dispute."

"I'd do it for you."

Ed took a step toward the mall office and turned. "I'll tell you what, Arlo. If she catches me, I'll cover for you, but I'm not hanging around." Ed backpedaled another step.

Arlo pointed at him. "Deal!"

The big man turned and walked away.

***

Security Officer Eileen Webster intercepted him and blocked his path. "Hold up there, handsome."

"Good morning, Eileen."

"I told you to be careful."

"That you did."

Her eyes dropped to the brown paper sack he carried. "Always with your lunch."

Ed looked down the hall but didn't see any police officers. He glanced over his shoulder to see that the mall walkers had swarmed Arlo.

"The cops are looking for you."

"So I heard." His attention returned to the

security officer. "What do they want?" he asked, but he already knew.

"Somebody robbed Hurley last night in the mall office. They took all the money from the fundraiser."

Ed had been involved in some heists while with the Satan's Dawgs. Robbing a mall fundraiser seemed a risky proposition for a low reward. "When did it happen?"

"After the mall closed. Hurley stayed late to count the money."

"By himself?"

She rolled her eyes. "You know how the man is. Doesn't trust anybody. Can't you just see him back there, counting all that money like a poor man's Scrooge? Probably even rolled in it."

Ed looked up and down the hallways of the mall. Still no cops were in sight. However, the mall walkers were now approaching. He faced Eileen again. "If the mall was closed, how'd someone get in to rob him? Better yet, how'd they get out?"

Eileen fingered the keys attached to her belt. "The way I figure the first part is the suspect must have hidden somewhere until the mall closed. Maybe the restrooms or the basement or one of the vacants."

"Aren't the vacant units locked?"

"They are. So is access to the basement, which we used to check every night, but now we got nobody to do that since Hurley fired our night watchman."

"Why'd he do that?"

Eileen shook her head. "Budget cuts. Look around. This whole place is operating on a shoestring. Until the end of the year, I'm a one-woman security team."

"That doesn't seem very smart."

Her eyes narrowed. "You saying I can't do the job?"

"I'm saying you need some help."

She flashed a crooked smile. "Okay, I'll give you that, but I'm more than enough man for the job."

Ed glanced around. "So, you think someone hid out until the mall closed."

"Almost certainly. And the next part is easy. After the doors were locked, they went to the office and conked Hurley over the head." She mimed the action.

"How'd they know Hurley was going to work late?"

Eileen shrugged. "How should I know? Maybe they didn't, and it was just a bonus to get to knock him about. He's got a big bruise on that side of his face. It's an improvement if you ask me. Then they took the money and walked out. Easy peasy."

"With all those jugs?" Ed remembered the sight of the pyramid of plastic jugs filled with coins and dollar bills. It didn't seem like something one person could quickly move. Even several men would have to make multiple trips.

Eileen shrugged. "It is what it is."

"Did you get it on camera?"

"Our system hasn't worked in over a year. The

mall is too broke to replace it." She shoved her hands in her pockets. "We leave it up for the illusion of security. I even told the cops as much. I knew it would come back and bite us in the butt someday. Guess that day is today."

Ed glanced up the hallway again. No cops were approaching.

The mall walkers passed now. As they did, Arlo smiled sheepishly and waved with his free hand. His wife held his other hand and tugged on it to hurry him along.

"Got to give them credit," Eileen said as the walkers continued by. "Every day, rain or shine, they're in here making the loops."

"What reason did the cops give for wanting to talk with me? Did Hurley say something?"

"It's because you're Santa." Eileen smacked his arm. "I told you this was bound to happen, and here we are—Christmas is ruined." She didn't seem upset by this latest revelation. Frankly, neither was Ed. The holiday was the least of his worries.

He asked, "What else have you heard?"

"Nothing," she said, "except I'm supposed to notify the cops when you arrive."

"I just got here."

"Then I'm in the clear. Guess I should call and let them know. They're waiting for you at the mall office. Are you going to run now?"

Ed's brow furrowed. "And go where? If the cops want to talk, they'll find me. Sooner or later, they always do. I might as well go down there and get it over with."

"Sounds like you've been to this rodeo before."

Ed shrugged. "Once or twice."

Eileen stepped aside. "Well, don't let me stop you, cowboy. Giddy up."

***

Two cops stood outside the entrance of the hallway leading to the mall office. Ed slowed as he approached, but they perked up when they noticed him. The younger of the two stepped forward. He had blond hair that was cut in a businessman's style.

"Ed Belmont?"

"That's right."

"We need to ask you some questions." The name tag on his blue uniform read *Duffy*. He eyed the brown paper sack Ed held. "What's in the bag?"

"My lunch."

Duffy extended his hand. "Care if I take a look?"

Ed handed him the sack, and the cop snatched it away. The officer stuck his hand in and rustled around. "What type of sandwich is that? Peanut butter and jelly?"

The older cop stepped forward now. He was heavier than his counterpart, with a thick mustache that drooped over his upper lip. His hair was cut in the flat-top style favored by soldiers. His name tag read *Lobdell*. "I've seen you around. Usually near that used bookstore on Main."

"I like books." It was still an odd statement for Ed to verbalize.

"Uh-huh. Well, you're a hard guy to forget." He glanced down to the back of Ed's hand. "I never noticed the tattoo before."

Officer Duffy pushed the sack back to Ed. "Where were you last night, about eleven?"

"At home."

"Anyone see you there?"

"My cat."

Duffy smirked. "We got us a funny man."

"A real comedian," Lobdell agreed.

"You two accusing me of something?"

Officer Lobdell stepped closer. "Should we accuse you of something, Mr. Funny Man?"

Cops, Ed thought. They were always playing the hard game when there was no need for it. He stepped back.

"No," he said. "It was me and the cat. That's it." Ed never even considered inviting them over to check out his apartment. Letting cops into your home was as bad as inviting a vampire in.

Duffy crossed his arms. "What did you and this supposed cat of yours do until you came here?"

"I read a book." He should have stopped there, but instead, he said, "You should try it sometime."

"I read," Duffy said.

Lobdell rolled his eyes.

Duffy noticed his partner's lack of respect and dropped his arms. "I do read. Lots of stuff."

"Yeah?" Ed asked. "What do you read?"

Officer Lobdell quickly held out his hand to stop his partner from speaking. "We're getting off track. According to you, you spent all night and this morning with a cat and a book."

"I slept, of course." Ed waggled the brown paper bag. "Then I made this. That doesn't happen all by itself."

Lobdell stepped forward again. "You don't seem too worried that two cops are asking you for an alibi. Don't you want to know why?"

"A couple people already told me what happened. You guys assume I did it."

"Did you?" Duffy asked.

Ed cocked his head. "I'd lose my job."

"You're a mall Santa," Lobdell said. "Not the kind of career choice people worry about hanging on to."

"And you still haven't said no," Duffy added.

"No," Ed said. "Is that clear enough? I did not assault anyone."

"What about the robbery?"

"I didn't do that either."

Lobdell's eyes narrowed. "Maybe we should go check out your apartment. See what we can see."

There it was, Ed thought. The vampires were at the door, asking to be invited in. He said, "You've got no probable cause."

Officer Lobdell chuckled and leaned toward his partner. "Look at this guy. From Mr. Funny Man to Mr. Probable Cause." Focusing on Ed again, he said, "You sound like a jail house lawyer. Been to prison, I take it. Is that where you got that tattoo?" He motioned toward the inky ball of fire.

The situation was spiraling quickly out of control, Ed thought. He needed to stop talking or he was likely to end up in hot water.

Duffy leaned in. "Not going to answer the man? Silence is guilt, you know."

"I thought silence was golden."

"Not in our world," Lobdell said. "Grab him, Duff. I'm gonna get the detective. We got our guy."

Chapter 7

Ed Belmont stood on the sidewalk in front of his apartment building and held his lunch sack with both hands. On either side of him were Officers Lobdell and Duffy. Ed wasn't in handcuffs. He'd gone willingly with the cops. What other choice was there?

While the three of them drove to his apartment, Ed tried to explain why there wasn't any way that he could have been the robber, but the two officers wouldn't listen. They kept telling him to save it for the detective.

A red patrol car pulled to the curb, and a heavyset cop exited. He wore a dark suit and white shirt. His black tie was too short, though, and it stopped at the apex of his belly. In his left hand was a notebook. He approached Officers Lobdell and Duffy.

"This the mook?"

"This is him," Lobdell proudly said. "Ed Belmont."

The detective studied Ed now with the gaze of a professional examiner. "How long have you had that tattoo on your hand?"

It was a question Ed hadn't expected. Most ask the meaning behind it or where he got it. He'd never been asked how long he'd had it. He didn't see any reason not to answer it truthfully. The truth was always the easiest to remember.

"About fifteen years."

Novak continued to study him. "I don't know. He don't look like no Santa. He seems too young. Too something else. You ever ride a motorcycle? You look like the type to ride a bike."

Ed shook his head. "Not me."

"What's in the brown paper?" The detective glanced at Lobdell. "You search the sack?"

"We did."

Officer Duffy added, "It's peanut butter and jelly."

Lobdell rolled his eyes. "This is the guy."

Duffy nodded. "Definitely him."

"Are you the guy?" the detective asked Ed.

"I'm not. That's what I've been trying to tell these two. If I was going to rob the mall, why did I come back to work?" He lifted the small sack. "Why'd I bring my lunch?"

"To keep things the way they are," Lobdell said. "Not to raise any suspicion."

"Maybe you just like peanut butter and jelly," Duffy added. "I do."

The detective's lips pursed, then moved side to side. When his eyes narrowed, he asked, "Do you know who I am?"

Ed shook his head.

"I'm Detective Stewart Novak." He swiped his jacket away from his hip to reveal a badge and gun. "Mind if we search your apartment?"

"Of course, I mind."

"See?" Lobdell said, but the detective shook his head to stop the officer from talking further.

"Why do you mind?" Novak asked.

"A man has a right to his privacy."

"Not when he's committing crimes."

Ed cocked his head. "You've got no proof of that. Besides, you're talking illegal search and seizure. It's in the constitution."

Lobdell clapped his hands once and faced the detective. "Did I tell you or did I tell you? Jail house lawyer."

Novak's eyes briefly narrowed. "So." It wasn't a question.

They were at a standoff, and both sides knew it. Now, it was time to see who blinked first. It wasn't going to be him. Ed crossed his arms, set his jaw, and glowered at the cops.

Novak nodded. "Just to confirm—you're not going to let us search?"

"Why should I?" Ed said. "I don't have to."

"Do you know why I'm here?"

"Because John Hurley said I assaulted him."

Novak shrugged a single shoulder. "He never mentioned you. When the responding officers asked about the mall Santa, he said he didn't like you, but he couldn't be sure it was you. He actually said he doubted it was you."

"Hurley said it wasn't me?"

"No," Novak said. "He said it was doubtful. That's why no officer went to your apartment this morning."

"Then why were these two so excited to grab me?"

"Anonymous caller," the detective said. "We got a call this morning who said you were the convenience store robber and the man responsible for robbing the mall. They also said we'd find evidence inside your apartment."

"Doesn't that seem suspicious?" Ed asked.

"A lot of things seem suspicious. How is that any more than anything else?"

"Well," Ed said, "I didn't rob anyone, and the only thing in my apartment is my cat."

Novak wiped a thumb across the tip of his nose. "So, I ask you again. Will you let us search your apartment?"

"Man or woman?"

The detective's brow furrowed. "What are you talking about?"

"The caller. Was it a man or a woman?"

"Doesn't matter. Are you going to let us search or not?"

"No," Ed said. "I did nothing wrong."

"That's what I figured." The detective turned to the two patrol officers. "Hold him here until I get back. I'm gonna get a warrant." He headed toward his patrol car.

Ed knew what would happen now. Novak would go back to the department and spend an hour or so writing up a search warrant. It would be filled with legal words and enough general suspicions that a cop-friendly judge would sign it. Then the detective would return to search Ed's apartment with the help of Lobdell and Duffy. All Ed would have done was waste a few hours of his life for the same result.

"Wait," he said.

Novak looked back over his shoulder.

Ed jerked his head toward his apartment.

The detective returned to where he previously stood. "Going to let us search now?"

"Looks like I have no choice."

"What changed your mind?"

"I can't hang around here all day. I've got to get to work."

Novak smirked. "For all those kids?"

Ed shrugged. "Since I didn't rob anyone, I need the paycheck." He again motioned toward the building. "You want to do this or not?"

The detective reached into his pocket and pulled out a little white card and a silver pen. "Sign this. It's your consent to search. Just so you can't change your tune later and say we didn't get your permission."

After Ed signed, he thrust the card back to the detective. Out of spite, he tried to keep the pen, but Novak snapped his fingers. Ed reluctantly gave it back.

The four of them entered the building and walked up to the second floor. Ed slipped his key into the lock. "I've got to warn you—" He looked back, and both Duffy and Lobdell put their hands on their guns. The two officers leaned forward expectantly.

"Relax," Ed said. "I was just warning you that the cat doesn't like cops."

"He's met a lot of them?" Novak asked.

"No, but he knows you guys work with dogs. That's enough to put him off the entire lot of you."

Ed turned the key, but he didn't feel the lock

move. He glanced back at Novak.

"Is there a problem?" the detective asked.

"I know I locked it when I left."

"You're saying it's unlocked?"

"That's what it felt like."

Lobdell chuckled. "Uh-huh. Likely story."

Duffy chimed in. "What do you want to bet we find something, and he uses this as an excuse? 'Somebody broke into my apartment.'" He whined and air-quoted that last bit.

Novak's gaze narrowed. "You going to do that, Belmont?"

"I don't know what's on the other side of the door."

"It's your apartment."

"I know I locked it."

Novak exhaled dismissively. "Step aside." The detective pushed Ed away. Then he twisted the knob and opened the door. When he stepped into the apartment, he announced, "Utopia Police Department, if anyone is in here, come out with your hands where we can see them."

"Should just be the cat," Ed said.

Novak snapped his fingers, and Lobdell pointed at the big man to be silent. Duffy held a finger to his lips and uttered a louder than necessary, "Shut it."

The detective further entered the apartment and stopped. "Well, well, well. What do we have here?"

Lobdell grabbed Ed by the arm and jerked him into the apartment.

Tossed in the middle of the small living room

were a crumbled Santa suit and a plastic jar filled with dollar bills and coins. Some of the money had spilled out on the floor.

Travis stood near the edge of the room. He eyed the unexpected visitors with unimpressed curiosity.

"Is that what I think it is?" Officer Duffy asked.

"Yeah," Ed said. "I told you there was a cat."

Novak turned around but thumbed toward the items on the floor. "Care to explain this?"

"The apartment was unlocked. Obviously, someone planted it."

Officer Lobdell chuckled. "You called it, Duff. Just what you said he would say."

Duffy whined and moved his hips side to side as he spoke. "Someone broke into my apartment and left me a Santa suit and a bucket full of money. Boo-hoo."

Detective Novak studied Ed. "That's your story, Belmont? You want us to believe another Santa is trying to frame you for his crimes?"

"That's right," Ed said. "That's exactly what I want you to believe. Because it's the truth."

"How naive do you take me to be?" Novak pulled his phone from his jacket and photographed the items in the middle of the room. When he lowered it, the detective said, "Put the suit on."

Ed cocked his head.

Novak's eyes hardened. "Put it on, or we'll arrest you right now and make you put it on down at the station."

For a moment, Ed wondered if he could fight his way out of this small room. He was reasonably sure he could take Officer Duffy and Detective Novak, but Lobdell would be a challenge. If it were just one-on-one, then it wouldn't be close. But three-on-one created specific problems. He'd fought his way out of situations like this before, but today didn't seem to be the right course of action. If all else failed, he could always call Marshal Goodspeed. However, that didn't need to happen—yet.

Ed grabbed the Santa jacket from the floor. "I want it noted that I'm doing this under protest."

"Jail house lawyer," Lobdell muttered.

"A regular Matlock from Cell Block D," Duffy added.

Novak spun his hand in a circle. "Stop stalling and put it on."

Ed took off his coat, then grabbed the Santa jacket. He slipped his arms into it and shrugged it on. The garment fit tight around his shoulders, but there was plenty of room around the midsection. Santa's generous belly would ensure that. However, the sleeves fell several inches short of his wrists.

Ed straightened to his full height and pulled his shoulders back. The sleeves pulled up even further.

Novak's grin faded, and his face soured.

"What the heck?" Lobdell said.

"Is it supposed to look like that?" Duffy asked. "He looks like he's wearing a kid-size."

The detective eyed the younger cop. "Zip it,

Duff." Novak turned his attention back to Ed. "Now, the pants."

Ed stretched his arms out in front of him, which pulled the sleeves halfway up to his elbows. "But the jacket—"

"The *pants*," Novak snapped. "Or we'll do it at the station."

Ed silently removed his boots and pants. It wasn't the first time he had disrobed in front of law enforcement officials. He had to do it anytime he entered jail or prison. It was a feeling he did not enjoy, though. Once he was down to his boxers, he grabbed the red pants and slipped them on.

The waist fit a little loose—Santa was a jolly sort, after all—but the pant legs stopped a couple of inches above his ankle.

"Would you look at that?" Lobdell muttered.

Ed extended his arms in a what-can-I-say gesture. "If the suit don't fit, you must acquit."

Novak took his phone from his pocket again and photographed Ed. "Wipe that stupid smile off your face, Belmont."

Ed tried, but he couldn't. "All you've got is an ill-fitting Santa suit and one jar of money. Where's the rest? Where's the gun used in the heist?"

Novak's face flattened, and he eyed the two other cops. "Fan out."

Lobdell searched around the bed. Duffy entered the bathroom.

Ed continued. "I'm just saying. That would really put the finger on me, Detective. Finding the rest of the money. Finding a gun with my fingerprints. I'd like to see that."

Novak moved into the kitchen to search through a cabinet. He turned back toward Ed. "You don't have a gun."

"That's what I'm saying."

The detective pointed to the Santa suit. "And that isn't yours."

"What gave you your first clue?"

Novak spun around and slammed the nearest cabinet shut. "How'd they get in this apartment?"

"I told you it was unlocked." He pointed at the door. "When we came in. Remember?"

The detective returned to where Ed stood. "Who else has a key?"

"As far as I know, just me and the landlord—Sorrel Babin. He also owns the bookstore downstairs."

"Does anybody else live on this floor?"

Ed nodded. "The landlord has the other place. So, it's just us."

"Could anyone else have gotten your keys?" Novak asked. "Are they ever out of your sight?"

"They're in my locker in the employee breakroom while I'm wearing the Santa suit."

Novak rubbed his mouth for a moment before calling out, "Lobdell. Duffy."

The older officer's head appeared from the furthest side of the bed. "Nothing under here."

Duffy stepped out of the restroom. "Nada."

The detective pointed at Ed. "Keep an eye on Belmont."

Both officers nodded.

"I'm going downstairs and have a conversation with the landlord. Maybe he can help us figure out just what the heck is going on."

"Want me to go with?" Ed asked.

The detective frowned. "No."

Ed shrugged. "I was trying to be helpful."

"Your kind of help, I can do without."

***

After the three cops left with the evidence from his apartment, Ed stood alone on the sidewalk. The door from Yesterday's Books opened, and Sorrell Babin stepped out. He was an older man that Ed guessed to be in his mid-seventies. He was stooped and wore a heavy sweater, corduroy pants, and soft leather shoes.

Sorrell's French accent had faded slightly from his years of being in America. "Mr. Belmont? Are you okay?"

Ed shrugged. "Good enough."

"That detective. He was rude."

"Just doing his job. They put on that act because they think it will get better cooperation."

Sorrell grunted. "I did not like him. How could he think you might be the Santa who has robbed the stores around town? I told him that you are gentle. Not the kind of man who could do such a thing."

Ed clapped Sorrell's shoulder. "Thank you.

Hey, did you see anyone go up to my apartment?"

Sorrell smiled kindly. "The detective also asked that, and I told him the same thing. I did not see anyone. I had customers, and you know how that can be. Sometimes it can get very busy. I also didn't hear anyone up there. When you walk about, the floors tend to creak. Maybe the person in your apartment was smaller and lighter than you."

"Did you tell the detective that?"

"I did."

Ed hadn't considered how a creaking floor might lend itself to an alibi, but now he was thankful that they did.

The landlord said, "May I change the subject to something happier?"

"Please."

"How do you like the Parker novel?"

"I liked it. I maybe liked Parker even more than Travis McGee."

Sorrell covered his heart. "Oh, do not let that be because of me." He had recommended *The Hunter* to Ed. "Travis McGee is a good man—a hero at heart, but Parker is a bad man—a selfish man. They are both interesting to read, but you should like Travis more. Always like the good guy more."

Ed smiled. "I'll take that into consideration."

"Do that. Now, I must go back inside. I am too old to stand in the cold and talk books. If you want to come inside, we can argue the merits of the anti-hero, and I will recommend a new book.”

Ed didn't understand the last part of his invitation, but he declined, nonetheless. “Some other time. I have to get to work.”

“As you wish,” Sorrell said and put his hand on the store's door. “I will have a recommendation for you the next time you come in.”

“I'll look forward to it.”

Chapter 8

"I heard the cops took you away," Susan Roskam said.

Ed shrugged. "Only to my apartment."

They were outside the hallway to the mall office. Susan wore a set of plush elf ears and an inflatable sweater that made her look like a snow globe. A large canvas bag hung from her shoulders.

"Baby, It's Cold Outside" played over the mall speakers.

Susan's eyes widened. "The mall walkers said the cops arrested you."

"They didn't arrest me; they *detained* me." He'd often heard cops make that silly distinction for years. It seemed to only matter to the police and the courts. To everyone else, it felt the same, especially if handcuffs were involved.

She threw her arms up. "Detained? How's that different than an arrest?"

"One is longer than the other, but the cops can mess with a person either way."

Concern washed over her face. "And they checked your apartment?"

"That's right."

"Since you're here, I'm assuming the cops didn't find anything?"

"Nothing that's going to get me into trouble."

Susan straightened. "So, I guess you really

didn't do it."

"Rob the mall? No. Definitely not."

Her eyes narrowed. "But I know you wanted to smack Hurley over the head."

"That's not a crime."

She smiled. "Thank God, since we've all thought about it." Susan slipped the canvas bag from her shoulder and stuffed it into Ed's hands. Inside was a clean Santa suit. Occasionally, Susan swapped out his suits. They tended to get smelly otherwise. "Time for work. Go inside the breakroom and get ready. There's already a line of kids waiting."

"I saw."

"Did you see how unruly they were? I told them one of your reindeer was sick, and you were running late."

"I guess it wouldn't look good to tell them Santa was getting braced by the local cops."

"It wouldn't." Susan spun Ed around and pushed him toward the breakroom. "Hurry up and change. I'll go stall the kids." She started down the hall. "Oh, and Ed."

"Huh?"

"Lighten up, will you? You were intense to begin with, but now..." She brought her palms up toward her chin, inhaling deeply as she did so. "It's Christmas. Think happy thoughts."

"Happy thoughts," he muttered and tried to figure out how someone broke into his apartment.

***

"Bring me a new computer," the boy said. He wore a puffy coat, blue jeans, and snow boots. Mittens dangled from clips attached to the ends of his sleeves. On his head was a puff ball hat.

His name was Tommy, and he must have been five years old. It was an easy name for Ed to remember because he had quickly labeled the kid as Terrible Tommy. Not only was the boy demanding, but he wiggled constantly and smelled of spoiled milk and other unpleasant kid odors.

This was the third kid since sitting on the large red throne, but Ed was still in a foul mood. The first two were also older kids with similar mercenary demands. He would give anything for a run of younger ones who simply gawked at him.

Tommy squirmed on Ed's knee before continuing. "It's gotta have an Intel dual-core processor, not that other one." The boy pushed his glasses up the bridge of his nose, then wiped his sleeve along his mouth. "Do you know what I'm talking about? That other processor is stupid. My dad says it's just as good, but it's not. He doesn't know anything. *Ray's World*— it's this YouTube channel I watch. Have you ever seen it? You should watch it. It's really funny. They have this one video about which blender is the best for smoothies. Anyway, *Ray's World* says Intel dual-core is the best. I've watched all of Ray's videos and— Are you paying attention, Santa?"

Ed blinked. His thoughts had drifted back to the cops and his apartment. He looked down at the boy. "A computer," he muttered.

"With an Intel processor," Tommy corrected and stabbed a finger into his palm. "Dual-core. This is important. Not the other one. Maybe you should write this down. My dad has to write everything down, too." The boy glared at his father. "He never gets anything right. I don't want you to forget like him."

"I can remember it," Ed said. "The computer is all you want?"

Terrible Tommy's head whipped back to him. "*Intel.* It's an Intel dual-core, but there's more. It has to have a five hundred gig SSD drive—"

Ed glanced up at Susan, who was giving the thumbs-up signal from behind the camera. From behind the velvet rope, the boy's father rolled his eyes and shook his head.

When Tommy started prattling on about something called a graphics card, Ed decided he'd heard enough. He hoisted the boy from his knee.

"A computer," Ed loudly proclaimed.

"Intel!" the kid shouted and wriggled in Ed's hands. His arms swung wildly, and the mittens clipped to his sleeves whirled around like little rotor blades. "Dual-core! Dual-core!"

Tommy's father covered his face with both hands.

Ed put Tommy on the ground and pushed him toward Susan. The boy stutter-stepped, planted a foot, and turned. He pointed like a cop after a running thief.

"An Intel!" Terrible Tommy hollered. "I want an Intel!"

"Hey!" Ed barked.

Everyone in the waiting line stopped talking, and a silence fell over the mall's center court. Tommy's father's head popped up from his hands like a groundhog sensing danger.

Susan's eyes widened, and she whispered a plaintive, "No."

"It's the Most Wonderful Time of the Year" could be heard from overhead.

Ed leaned forward in his chair and rested an elbow on his knee. His already gravelly voice lowered another octave. "Are you yelling at Santa?"

It was a silly thing to ask, but Ed needed to establish some boundaries with these kids. As the bookkeeper for the Satan's Dawgs, no one ever dared to speak at him that way. He was done letting some snot-nosed kid get away with it.

The color drained from Tommy's face.

Several children in line clasped their parent's legs. Susan glanced nervously toward Tommy's father, who eagerly watched the interaction between his son and Santa.

Ed scooted toward the edge of his chair and crooked his finger. Tommy hesitatingly stepped forward.

"Do you want to be on the naughty list? This close to Christmas might cost you a bunch of presents. Maybe get you a lump of coal. How'd you like that, Tommy?"

The kid slowly shook his head.

Ed motioned toward the boy's father. "How about I tell him you want a football instead? Would you like that?"

The boy's eyes widened. "No."

Ed's brow furrowed, and his lip curled. "No, what?"

Tommy swallowed with some difficulty, then squeaked out, "No, sir."

"I told some other kid he was getting a football. He wasn't happy about it either, but guess what he's getting for Christmas now?"

Tommy whispered, "A football?"

"That's right. A football. So, we understand each other?"

The boy nodded.

"Are you ever going to yell at Santa again?"

Tommy shook his head. "No, sir. Never, sir."

"Get out of here." Ed leaned back and announced, "He wants a computer."

"With an Intel processor," the boy muttered as he walked toward his father.

"Merry Christmas!" Susan called.

The crowd of nearby parents exclaimed, "Merry Christmas!" Their children, however, were suspiciously quiet.

***

Raleigh Dunham shoved his hands into the pockets of his workman's slacks. He was in his late fifties and stood an inch under six feet with thinning hair and a flushed complexion. The buttons on his shirt struggled to contain his ample belly. On his belt were a heavy clip of keys. "Heard you had some commotion with an unruly kid."

"There was no problem," Susan said. "Everything is fine."

"That's not what I heard."

Ed reclined in Santa's throne and ignored Raleigh. The guy smelled of grease, cheap alcohol, and body odor. He seemed the type to need more attention than was necessary.

The line of nearby kids and parents waited anxiously. The maintenance man had cut to the front and interrupted the flow of business. Until now, Ed and Susan had been humming along nicely. They were down to six kids, and Ed had hopes they could get it to zero—something he hadn't been able to accomplish yet. With this interruption, the line would surely repopulate with children. Kids were like weeds, Ed thought. No matter how many times you thought you got rid of them, they kept coming back.

Raleigh motioned toward Ed. "I heard he pulled a Chet."

"No, he didn't. Chet was good with kids." Susan quickly added. "But so is Ed. The parents love him."

The maintenance man chuckled. "And they're the ones buying the pictures, am I right?"

Susan's face flattened. "What do you want, Raleigh?"

"Nothing. I'm just checking on you guys." He

glanced around before continuing. "You know, to make sure everything is working correctly."

"What's there to fix?" Susan asked. "We got a chair, and we got the camera. Nothing that's gonna break."

"You never know." Raleigh motioned toward the tree. "Maybe the tree could fall down, and you would need me to put it back up. That sort of thing could happen."

Ed eyed Raleigh now. "Are you threatening us?"

Raleigh's gaze landed on the big man. "Huh?"

"Because," Ed said, leaning forward, "that sounds like what you're doing."

"Is that true, Raleigh?" Susan asked.

The maintenance man chuckled nervously and touched his chest with both hands. "Who am I to threaten anything? I work here. Remember? I'm just asking if things are working all right. Sheesh. Don't get so touchy, Santa."

Ed stood and looked down at Raleigh. He lowered his voice to a whisper. "I've been threatened before."

"By who?" Raleigh asked. "The Grinch?" He snickered and glanced around. Realizing no one was nearby to hear his joke, Raleigh slowly returned his gaze to Ed. "Relax, man. Sheesh. I'm only trying to avoid Hurley."

"Why?"

"Why not?" Raleigh covered his mouth with his hand and burped. "He's always got me doing little errands. Fix this, move that. I was hoping you two might have something simple for me to do, but I can take a hint."

"Can you?" Ed asked.

Raleigh nodded. "Oh, yeah. I don't need to be told twice. Let me get on with my life, and you can get back to what you do best."

"You do that," Ed said.

The maintenance man shuffled away but glanced back over his shoulder as he went.

"What do you think he was trying to do?" Susan asked.

Ed shrugged. "Who knows? But he should cut down on the drinking at work."

***

"So, this thing," Ed said, "you do what with it?"

The little girl—her name was Becca—mashed her fingers together. "You pop it."

"And it's a toy?"

Becca nodded so forcefully that her stocking cap slipped down her head. Ed moved it back into place.

"What's it called again?"

"A Fidget Popper." The girl laughed. "A Fidget Popper!"

Her father stood near the velvet rope. His eyes widened at hearing the girl's words, and he shook his head.

Ed leaned down. "Why do you want this?"

"Because it makes noise." Becca mashed her fingers together again. "Pop. Pop pop. Pop!" Her head bounced from side to side. "Pop. Pop pop.

Pop!"

"You like toys that make noise?"

"Uh-huh. Pop. Pop pop. Pop!"

Ed glanced up to check out the father again, but now another man stood next to him. The newcomer was short, with a long, white beard that covered most of his face. He wore a red ski jacket that struggled to hide his rather large belly. He scowled at Ed.

"And I want some maracas," Becca said. She waggled both hands back and forth.

Susan noticed Ed's gaze and traced it to the bearded man. She hurried over and said something to the newcomer.

"Maracas," the girl said again. "The things that go *sh-sh-sh-sh.*"

The man with the white beard faced Susan, and they exchanged several heated words. As their conversation continued, the man's face reddened. He angrily poked Susan's blow-up snow globe sweater. When he finally walked away, Susan appeared shaken.

Becca said, "Santa?"

Ed looked down. "Uh-huh. I heard you. Noisemaker."

"*Sh-sh-sh-sh.* Pop. Pop pop. Pop!"

He lifted the girl and set her on the ground. To her father, he announced, "She wants a drum kit."

Becca's face lit up, and she pumped her fist. "Yes!" The girl ran toward her father, who appeared stricken by bad news.

Ed waved Susan over. "Who was that?"

She took a final glance over her shoulder. "That was Chet Malone—your predecessor."

"He didn't look happy."

Susan frowned. "He's not. Like I said before, he's a bit of a loon. Gave me all sorts of indigestion."

"What about?"

Susan shook her head. "Where to begin? But now's not the time. We've got kids in line."

"Nine," Ed said. "We've got nine kids."

A smile returned to her face. "Somebody sounds like he's finally getting into the Christmas spirit! I'll go get the next one."

When she hurried off, Ed fell backward into his throne.

Chapter 9

"So, they brought you to your apartment and did a search?" Marjorie Lewis asked. "How rude."

Ed bit into his peanut butter and jelly sandwich. It was only his second bite. He hadn't told Marjorie that the cops took him to his apartment, nor that Detective Novak searched through his stuff. She'd heard all that through the grapevine.

"Are you okay?" she asked.

He shrugged and continued chewing. He could have swallowed but figured why not continuing working on the sandwich. It was better than talking with the attractive and unrelenting Marjorie. In his previous life, Ed would have humored her, but he didn't want to do that now. He had Daphne Winterbourne on his brain.

"If something like that happened to me," she leaned in and looked at Ed with earnest sincerity. "I'd be afraid to go home. Is that what you're feeling?"

"No."

Marjorie wore another brightly colored dress. A pink sweatband wrapped around her head, and a row of bracelets clattered about her left wrist. A single ponytail rose and fell from the left side of her head.

"Maybe you should come over to my house," Marjorie said. "I could make you some dinner. Something real nice. I make a mean cannelloni."

"No."

"I guess I could come to your place and cook. I don't know what ingredients you've got available, but—"

"No." Ed jammed his sandwich back into this mouth.

"Maybe we could get a pizza."

"I said no."

Marjorie's shoulders slumped. "But I haven't got to sit on your lap and tell you what I want for Christmas."

"You're not going to sit on my lap."

"Whatever. I'll sit on your knee."

"No, you won't. And I don't want to know what you want for Christmas."

"But you're Santa," she whined. "And I've been good."

The door to the breakroom opened, and John Hurley entered. He wore black pants, black shoes, and a salmon-colored shirt. His bruised face slackened when he saw Marjorie.

She twisted in her chair and eyed the newcomer. "He's not taking private requests."

"What?"

Marjorie motioned toward Ed. "Him. He's on break."

Hurley said, "That's good because I came to talk."

"You'll have to wait your turn. We're in the middle of something here." Marjorie waggled a finger between her and Ed. "Come back in a few."

The manager eyed Ed, who slowly shook his head.

"Marjorie," Hurley said. "I'd like to talk with Ed—alone."

She trained her gaze on Ed but held two fingers up. "A couple of minutes. We're almost done."

Ed swallowed the bite of sandwich he'd been working on. "She's leaving."

Marjorie's brow furrowed. "I am?"

"That's right."

Hurley stepped deeper into the breakroom.

"But why do I have to go?" Marjorie eyed the two men with some suspicion. In a moment, her face brightened. "Oh, I get it. Secret Santa stuff."

Ed's face pinched again. He did that a lot around Marjorie.

"Say no more." She stood and smiled brightly. "I'll let you boys get to it." As she passed the mall manager, she whispered loud enough for Ed to hear. "Let me know when you're done. Ed and I still have unfinished business—if you know what I mean."

When the door to the breakroom closed, Hurley turned to him. A large bruise covered the left side of his face. "The cops didn't arrest you."

Ed dropped the remaining portion of his sandwich onto the brown paper bag. "You know it wasn't me."

"It was you."

"But you told the cops it wasn't me."

Hurley feigned innocence. "Did I say that?"

Ed cocked his head. "They said you didn't think it was me."

"The more I've thought about it, the more I think it was you." Hurley pointed at Ed. "No other Santa has it out for me."

"Maybe not Santa." Ed crossed his arms. "But a lot of people have it out for you."

The mall manager appeared surprised at that statement. "Who? Who has it out for me? Name one."

"Every store owner in the mall."

"They don't count. Name another."

"Your employees."

"They don't count either."

"The cops didn't like you. Maybe one of them smacked you around."

Hurley rolled his eyes. "They didn't know me until today."

"Still," Ed said, "you might be the least likeable person in Utopia."

"I don't need to be likeable to do my job."

"Maybe this had nothing to do with you."

That gave Hurley pause. "Of course, it has to do with me. Why else would someone hit me?"

Ed stared at him.

"This was totally about me. This was personal." He pointed at his face. "How can you not see that?"

"Maybe they just wanted the money. Maybe you were just the guy who got in the way."

The mall manager's eyes widened. "Are you

always this dense? They hit me. Me! This is all about me!”

Ed imagined punching Hurley. It was a satisfying vision. Maybe it really was about him.

“What did you do with the money?” Hurley asked.

“I didn’t rob you. I didn’t rob the mall. Ask the cops.”

“Maybe they don’t believe you did it, but I do.” He bent slightly forward. “I do.”

“If you believe that, why am I still here?”

Hurley’s eyes narrowed. “Because you don’t work for me. You work for her. If you did work for me, trust me, you’d be gone in a heartbeat.”

“What did I ever do to you?”

Hurley scoffed. “You’re a mall Santa. You can’t do anything to me.”

“You just said I hit you and robbed you.”

The mall manager waved his comment away. “Other than that.”

“I’ve gotten under your skin.”

“No, you haven’t.”

“Yes, I have.”

Hurley’s face reddened. “No, you haven’t.”

“The funny thing,” Ed said, “is I have no idea how I did it.”

“Some people just don’t like some people.” The mall manager headed for the door. He stopped just before opening it. “And stay away from our store owners.”

“You mean Marjorie?”

“Who else?”

“Why? Do you like her? Is that what this is

about?"

Hurley faced him again. "No, I do not like her. The Superior Mall is a wholesome enterprise."

"Wholesome?"

"That's right. A lot of other malls might be like Club Med, but not this one, mister. Keep your testosterone to yourself."

Hurley yanked open the door and stepped outside.

Once alone, Ed bit into his sandwich. Just a day ago, dealing with the kids was his biggest worry. Now he had an angry mall manager to deal with and the cops sniffing around. Could things get any worse?

Marjorie hurried in, and fate answered that question for him.

She quickly closed the door behind her. "Hurley walked right by and didn't bother to tell me you guys were done. So rude. What's going on with him anyway?"

"Nothing," Ed said through a mouthful.

"He looked mad. Did you do that to him?"

"He's fine."

"If you say so." She sat at the table and leaned toward Ed again. "Now, where were we?"

"I don't remember."

Marjorie's face brightened. "Oh, yeah. Let me sit on your lap."

"No."

She giggled. "You're so funny."

***

After his lunch, Ed went for a walk. There weren't many places a man dressed as Santa could go without attracting attention. Had Marshal Goodspeed considered that before assigning him to this job and city? She seemed excited that he could hide behind the beard and gloves. On the surface, that was a good idea.

However, children and their parents were immediately drawn to him. Worse, he stood out like a sore thumb. Everyone noticed him while walking through the mall. It was unlikely that a member of the Satan's Dawgs or a sister club would be in the Superior Mall. But an affiliate might. Plenty of folks hung around the club and helped the members gain access to legitimate society. Often those were women, and it didn't take much glancing around to know that most of the shoppers at the mall were of the finer sex.

Ed calmed down by reminding himself that most of them would never have seen the mob's website. They would have no idea that Ed was on the run. He was the only one worried that anyone would recognize him.

To distract himself from his worries, he'd taken to counting how many vacant spaces were inside the mall. He was up to fifteen when a man called out from behind him.

"Hey, big dog. Don't think you're fooling anyone in that costume."

Ed stiffened and slowed his walk. *Big dog* could be a harmless term, but it could also reference his former club.

"That's right," the man said. "I'm talking to

you."

The mall wasn't full, but there were still plenty of folks around—children, too. Whoever was calling him out wouldn't risk trying anything here and now. Would they?

Ed glanced over his shoulder. He was prepared to strike or dart to the side, whatever was dictated by what awaited him. When he saw his pursuer, he smiled.

"What's so funny?" Chet Malone asked.

"Nothing."

Chet's red ski jacket was now opened and revealed a threadbare white t-shirt. He rubbed a chubby hand over his white beard. "I think you're laughing at me."

"I wouldn't do that."

"Whatever." Chet's gaze traveled his length. "Nobody believes you're really Santa in that outfit. You look like Bigfoot decided to get in the Christmas spirit. Santa can't dunk a ball or fight Godzilla."

"What do you want, Chet?"

The older man took a half-step back. "You know my name? I'm flattered."

"Your reputation precedes you."

Chet chuckled. "Well then, you should know not to mess with me. I'm not a man to be trifled with."

"I'm not the trifling type," Ed said. "What do you want?"

"I want my job, and you've got it."

"Not going to happen."

Chet reached for Ed's beard, but the bigger

man smacked his hand away.

"That's not even a real beard."

"It's real enough."

Chet tugged on his own facial hair. "I don't have to wear a falsie."

"I need to go," Ed said. He started to turn, but Chet grabbed his arm.

Ed's eyes dropped to the hand wrapped around his bicep. Maybe it was the costume, perhaps it was that the beard hid most of his face, but Chet wasn't concerned by Ed's scowl. Instead, Chet said, "Don't turn from me, big dog. We still got business."

"We don't have any business. Aren't you banned from the mall?"

"I'm not banned." Chet glanced around. "I was asked to leave, and that was just because of a misunderstanding."

"Let go," Ed said.

"Walk away from the job. It's mine."

"Susan doesn't want you." Ed lowered his voice. "Let go. I'm warning you."

"You're warning me? That's rich. And Susan will take me back if she knows what's good for her."

"Did you just threaten Susan?"

"No, I—"

Ed punched Chet in the chest. The white-haired man released his grip around Ed's arm and fell to the floor.

Ed stepped forward and pointed at the man on the ground. "Two things, Chet. First, don't ever touch me again. Second, don't ever threaten Susan. Got it?"

Chet rubbed his chest. "I got it," he wheezed. "I got it."

As Ed walked away, he overheard a little boy ask his mother in an astonished tone, "Did you see Santa hit that man? What do you think he asked for?"

Chapter 10

Susan Roskam whispered into Ed's ear. "You slugged Chet?"

He nodded.

Ed sat on Santa's throne and counted the line of kids. Seven.

Not too bad, but it looked like a father and mother were approaching with a gaggle of five more. Why did some parents do that to themselves? Did they think so little of their own lives that they needed to fill it with children to distract from their misery? The large family joined the line.

Susan's face tightened with anger, but she kept her voice low. "Why would you hit him? You can't do that sort of thing. It's bad for business."

"Twelve."

"Huh?"

Ed motioned toward the line. "There are twelve kids now."

"Yeah, fine, whatever," she whispered. Her face reddened, and she bent closer. The inflatable snow globe sweater she wore bumped Ed.

He leaned away from her.

"You can get in a lot of trouble for hitting him," Susan continued. "That's the sort of stupid things Chet did. Now, you're doing the same.”

“I did it one time. It’s not a habit, so relax. Go get one of the kids, and let’s get started.”

Several of the children in line waved at Ed. He grunted in response.

“No,” she whispered. “We’re not done with this conversation. The cops just talked to you this morning and now this. Are you looking for trouble?”

“I didn’t rob anyone, so I have nothing to worry about with the cops.”

“Still. There’s Hurley you’ve got to worry about. If he finds out about this, who knows what he’ll do?”

Ed eyed her. “What do you want from me?”

“Aren’t you going to apologize?”

“To Chet?”

Susan’s eyes bulged. “To me.”

“For what?”

“For all the drama you’re creating. You’re giving me heartburn.”

“Okay, fine. I apologize.”

Susan put her hands on her hips. “You don’t mean it.”

“I did nothing wrong.” A thought occurred to him. “How’d you find out I hit Chet?”

“Eileen told me. She saw it on the camera. And if you’re going to apologize, you should mean it.”

“I thought Eileen said the mall cameras didn’t work.”

“Maybe they’re working now. So, you’re not going to apologize?”

"You said not to do it if I didn't mean it."

"So, that's a no." Susan tsked. "Then tell me why you hit him."

"Chet wanted his job back."

She scoffed. "Not going to happen."

"That's what I told him."

"You hit him for that? I would have popped him earlier if that was the case."

Another family approached. This one had three kids with them. Several people in the crowd looked anxiously at the approaching group.

"Fifteen," Ed muttered.

Without looking back, Susan whispered, "We'll get to them soon enough."

"They're looking restless."

Susan rubbed the snow globe on her belly. "Chet wanting his job back was no reason to hit the man."

"You already said that."

"I want to make sure you heard it."

"Fine. I hear you."

She continued rubbing the snow globe portion of her sweater. "So, why did you hit him?"

"He threatened me."

"Oh." Her hand stopped its circular motion.

"I was going to let it slide, but then he threatened you."

Susan covered her mouth.

"That's when I punched him."

"Because he threatened me?"

"That's what I said."

She pshawed. "Well, why didn't you say that to begin with? That seems totally reasonable." Susan glanced over her shoulder. "Are you ready for a kid? Let's get you a kid." With that, she walked away.

***

"There's a rumor going round," John Hurley said as soon as he entered the breakroom.

Ed removed the Santa jacket. "Let me guess. It's got something to do with me."

"You assaulted a shopper."

"I didn't assault anyone."

Hurley put his hands on his hips. "That's not what I heard."

"You said it was a rumor."

"If I find out that you did—"

Ed dropped the Santa jacket onto a nearby chair. He still wore the Santa pants and boots. He crossed his arms and scowled at the mall manager. "What are you going to do about it?"

"You're out of here."

"What if it was in self-defense?"

"Are you admitting that you assaulted someone?"

"I'm not admitting anything. I'm asking a question. If it was in self-defense, would you give me a fair shake?"

Hurley squinted but didn't answer Ed's question.

"I see how it is."

The manager nodded. "That's how it is."

"What did I ever do to you?"

Hurley motioned toward Ed. "It's probably your face."

Ed furrowed his brow. "What's wrong with my face?"

"It bugs me."

"You bug me."

"Clever."

"Do you want to know what I think?"

"Why would I want to know what goes on in that meatball factory?"

"I think you're trying to pin the heist on me because you don't like me."

The mall manager laughed. "The heist? Who are you? James Cagney?"

Ed knew who the old-time actor was from watching a couple of black and white movies with his grandmother. He didn't remember them being heist films, but he was young at the time and didn't pay attention to those types of things.

"And don't try to distract from the situation," Hurley said. "If I find any proof that you were involved in an altercation with a customer, both you and Susan are gone."

"Don't take any pleasure in it."

He smiled. "Oh, I'll take great pleasure in it."

***

Ed found her scolding a teenager near the mall's exit.

Eileen Webster held a skateboard in her left

hand. Her right index finger waggled as she spoke. "Do you know how dangerous it is to ride this inside the mall?"

The kid was roughly fifteen and wore a black Pittsburgh Penguins jersey, baggy jeans, and Vans tennis shoes. His long hair flopped around his head as he nodded.

"Gimme my board." He reached for the skateboard.

Eileen twisted away.

"I'm trying to talk with you about safety."

"That's mine," the teenager said and grabbed Eileen's wrist.

She counter-grabbed the kid's arm, stepped to the side, and flipped him to his back. The teenager let out a whoosh of air.

"As I was saying, it's dangerous to ride this in the mall. Do you understand?"

The kid nodded.

"I can't hear you," Eileen said.

"Uh-huh," he moaned.

"What should I do with you?"

"You could let me go."

Eileen noticed Ed approaching and lifted her chin in acknowledgment. She turned back to the kid. "I could do that. I could let you go, but what would you learn?"

The teenager struggled to his feet. "I've learned my lesson. I promise."

She eyed Ed. "What do you think?"

He shrugged. "He's a kid, and it's a skateboard."

"It's a gateway ride," she said. "First, it's this,

and then it's a BMX bike. Before long, he's in a motorcycle gang being a menace to society."

Ed didn't believe that was necessarily true, but he couldn't argue with her either. In his youth, he had muddled around on a skateboard that his grandmother bought for him. That happened until he found a BMX bike. Technically, he stole the bike since he knew its owner and where it belonged, but the kid often left it unguarded in his front yard overnight. The guy was practically begging for it to be stolen. At least, that was how the younger version of Ed rationalized it.

When the bike came up missing, the kid didn't seem too worried about it. After Ed rode the BMX through the neighborhood, the boy even commented that the bike looked like his. That's as far as the threat of recovery went. Soon, the boy was riding a new bike and leaving that one unattended in his front yard as well. Ed took that as tacit approval for his keeping the stolen BMX.

"So?" Eileen said. "If we give the skateboard back to this kid, are we going to be responsible for unleashing a monster on society?"

Ed motioned toward the teenager. "Where are your parents?" He surprised himself that he uttered the question and glanced around in sudden embarrassment. Being Santa was wreaking havoc on his cool meter.

"For real?" the teenager asked.

Eileen hugged the skateboard to her hip. "Yeah, what *was* that?"

"Give the kid the board."

She looked at him. "Look at you, Mr. Softy. If you want me to give him the board, I'll give him the board."

"Why are you making this about me?" Ed asked.

"Because I need to blame someone. Might as well be you." Eileen turned to the teenager and pushed the skateboard to him. "If I catch you around here again..."

"You won't." The kid snatched the skateboard and ran out of the mall.

"No skateboarding in the parking lot!" Eileen hollered.

The teenager tossed the board to the ground and hopped on it. One foot propelled him quickly away.

"Fat lot of good that did," she muttered. Turning to Ed, she said, "Heading home?"

"In a minute. You said the cameras weren't working."

Eileen frowned. "When did I say that?"

"You said that when we talked about the break-ins. You made some comment about it coming back to haunt you."

She nodded in recollection. "I guess I did say that, didn't I?"

"Then you told Susan you saw me hit Chet Malone on the cameras. Which is it?"

"I saw you hit Chet on the camera."

Ed spread his hands wide in a there-you-go gesture. "You see my dilemma."

"I misspoke."

"So, the cameras are working?"

"Of course, but the recording portion is not. We can watch what's going on in the mall, but we can't record any of it. So far, it's not been that big of a deal, but since we can't record it—"

"You really didn't record the fundraising heist?"

Eileen frowned. "Are you calling me a liar?"

"No. I'm trying to get it straight in my head. It's strange that the cameras aren't able to record, and the mall doesn't have any security staff working after it closes."

"I already told you—budget cuts. I don't make that decision. Hurley does."

"Yeah, Hurley. Mind if we look at those cameras?"

Eileen's thumb played with a space on her belt where a set of keys had been. "I don't have time. I'm on my rounds now."

"How long will that take? I'll wait."

"You're a suspicious one, aren't you?"

"I'm the one accused of hitting Chet."

"But I saw you hit him."

"I barely tapped him. It was more like a push. Maybe even a tap."

"Right."

"Got any proof that it happened otherwise?"

Eileen's grin was sly. "No, I don't. Come by sometime tomorrow, and I'll show you the cameras. You can prove to yourself that they aren't recording."

She started toward the opposite end of the mall.

Ed stayed there for a moment as he tried to piece it all together.

Chapter 11

It was after nine when Ed finally left the mall. Snow lightly fell as he headed back toward his apartment. He pulled the collar up on his coat, bowed his head, and stuffed his hands in his pockets. It was colder out than he expected.

Christmas was only a couple of days away, and this gig would soon end. That meant that Marshal Goodspeed would return with a new job for him. She'd been so excited about this one that he had some legitimate fears that the next one might be as the Easter Bunny.

No, Ed thought, that was in April. And they didn't have the bunny around for as long as Santa. But Goodspeed might still be obsessed with the costume idea. What other holidays were between now and then? Martin Luther King's Birthday. Valentine's Day. President's Day. St. Patrick's Day. None of them offered an opportunity to dress up in costume. Well, St. Paddy's did, but a leprechaun wouldn't hide his size or tattoos, and that was only for a single day. No, Goodspeed would need something else.

Up ahead, Ed saw the teenager from the mall with the Pittsburgh Penguins jersey. He stood on the corner with his skateboard in his hand. He didn't have a coat or hat on and might catch a cold. Ed shook the thought from his head. He'd been around too many kids the past several weeks.

When the light changed, the boy ran across the street and into the distant neighborhood. The Penguins jersey disappeared into the night.

Penguins, Ed thought, and he grunted in dismay. That's what Goodspeed would think about. Not the bird, but the sports team. She'd think about mascots. After the success of this Santa experience, she'd next want to dress him up as some symbol of a minor league baseball team. It would be some horrible mascot like Willie the cockatoo or Oliver the otter. Ed would spend his days running up and down the first-base line between innings, throwing t-shirts to drunken fans.

But that might require him to travel with the team. Did mascots go with their teams to road games? He didn't think so, but what if they did? Even if it were for only the occasional promotional deal, that sort of thing would needlessly expose Ed to new cities and new people. Goodspeed had a mean streak in her, but she wasn't careless.

Ed was lost in thought as he left the sidewalk and crossed the parking lot for the Quik N Go. Inside, a country-rap song played. The lyrics sounded as if the singer was extolling the virtues of gator wrestling.

Behind the counter, Nathan the clerk stared ahead with wide eyes. Ed nodded casually at the Santa Claus standing in the middle of the store. Before the bearded man could respond, Ed turned and headed toward the coolers.

His internal argument continued. Besides holiday figures and team mascots, what other opportunities were there for Ed to wear a costume? Superheroes did, and he'd rather go back to prison than wear his underwear on the outside of a pair of tights. What about ninjas? Outside of schlocky movies, he couldn't think of a reason to wear the black pajamas. It seemed the excuses to don a costume were limited.

He had to give it to Marshal Goodspeed. The Santa costume was the best of them all. Nothing else allowed him to hide in plain sight and not worry about being noticed. At this time of year, Santa seemed to be everywhere.

Ed yanked open a cooler door. He was in the mood for another Big Time burrito. He'd developed a particular appreciation for the mammoth meal. They weren't the healthiest things in the world to eat, but he was still in decent shape, and he didn't snack throughout the day. Ed figured he could make allowances for something like that.

He snatched one of the frozen burritos and stepped back to let the door close by itself. In the reflection of the cooler's glass, Ed saw him then—a gun-wielding Santa Claus.

Ed turned around.

The guy in the middle of the store was a nice-looking Father Christmas. The beard and suit fit him well. He swung around and pointed the gun at him. "Stay where you are, big fella."

"You got it."

"Get those hands where I can see them."

Ed lifted his burrito.

With Santa's attention diverted, Nathan never moved. His misty eyes stared at the red-suited interloper.

Over the store's radio, country-rapper sang about gigging frogs with his dog.

To Nathan now, Santa over his shoulder said, "Hurry up with that money."

"Uh, sure, man," the clerk said, which brought St. Nick's attention fully back to him. "Whatever you say." The cash register dinged before Nathan tugged open the drawer. "It's gonna be a little light. I already made the drop."

"Enough with the chatter," Santa said. He faced Nathan, now. "And throw in a carton of smokes."

The clerk's eyes narrowed. "Got a brand preference?"

"Marlboro reds."

"Huh."

"What?"

"We don't have any more of those in cartons."

Santa thrust his gun forward. "Then pick another. I don't care!"

The clerk's shoulders rose around his head.

Father Christmas glanced back at Ed. "What are you looking at?"

What he had been looking at was a mark at St. Nick's wrist. When he thrust his gun forward, the skin between the gloves and the red sleeve was exposed. Ed couldn't be sure of what it was. Maybe it was a smudge of grease, but perhaps it was a tattoo.

"Well?" Santa asked.

"You're famous," Ed said. "It's hard not to stare."

St. Nick swung the gun toward Ed, but the big man didn't flinch. He simply waggled the Big Time burrito in a hello fashion.

"Got some guts on you," Santa grunted. "Want to be a hero?"

Ed shook his head. "Not me."

"Remember that."

"Excuse me?" Nathan interrupted. "Mr. Santa?"

St. Nick swung the gun back toward the clerk.

Nathan flinched again then lifted three off-brand cartons. "Will these work? They're on special right now. Buy two get the third free."

"In the bag," Santa said. "C'mon, man! Are you trying to keep me here until the cops show up?"

Nathan ducked once more. "Not me." He hurriedly shoved the three cartons into Santa's bag then pushed it across the counter.

St. Nick snagged the canvas bag, took a step toward the door, and pointed the gun at Ed.

The multi-colored strip along the door jamb showed the red-suited robber stood roughly five-foot-seven.

"Am I gonna have a problem with you?" Santa asked.

Ed cocked his head. "Not me."

"In that case, Merry Christmas and to all a good night." Santa burst through the door and sprinted around the corner.

***

"You're giving me heartburn, Belmont," Detective Stewart Novak said.

"You're the second person to tell me that today."

"Maybe you should take that into consideration."

Ed shrugged.

The two men stood outside the convenience store. As protocol would dictate in a situation like this, Novak had insisted that Ed and Nathan be separated until the detective could interview them both. The detective didn't want their stories cross-contaminated. He'd already interviewed the clerk who was back inside the building.

Ed had just relayed his version of the events when Novak accused him of giving him acid reflux.

"The kid said you walked right by Santa," the detective said. "You didn't even pause to take him in."

"I see the suit every day."

"That's your excuse?"

Ed shrugged again. "What can I say? I had other things on my mind."

"Care to share?"

"I was thinking about what to eat."

The detective motioned toward the Big Time burrito that Ed still held. "And that's what you chose for dinner?"

"They're good. You should try one."

"Any distinguishing characteristics?"

Ed looked at the packaged burrito. "Refried beans, ground beef, lotsa cheese."

Novak's face tensed. "About Santa."

"White beard, red suit, black boots."

The detective crossed his arms and frowned. "Anything that might be of help?"

"He's five-seven." Ed pointed at the door. "They got a height strip in there. I caught it when he walked out."

Novak nodded. "We caught that on footage from one of his other robberies, but thanks for confirming it. You're a regular civic patron."

Ed didn't appreciate the sarcasm.

"Any other distinguishing marks or characteristics?"

"I was at the back of the store. What could I see?"

He could have told him about seeing the mark on the man's wrist, but what could he say to him beyond that? He didn't know for sure that it was a tattoo, and he didn't appreciate the detective's sarcasm. Ed kept this info to himself, but there was something he didn't mind sharing with Novak.

"I will tell you this much," Ed said. "You might want to look into Chet Malone."

The detective pulled his shoulders back and studied Ed. "And who is Chet Malone?"

"He's a former mall Santa. The guy here tonight is about the same height."

"You think this guy tonight might have been him?"

"Not really."

"Then why bring him up?"

Ed thought of something Arlo said. "All of us Santas look alike."

Novak's eyes widened. "Oh, no. You're not going to accuse me of that. That's profiling."

"But that's what you guys did with me."

"Not true. You had proximity to the crime, and we had an anonymous tip."

"Uh-huh."

Novak shook his head. "Don't give me that uh-huh garbage. We don't profile here in Utopia. We do honest police work. Maybe you're not used to seeing it, but that doesn't make it any less true."

Ed watched a passing car go by. "Maybe you should look at Chet Malone for the robbery of the mall, too."

"More profiling? No, thanks. I'll pass."

"Malone's jealous that I took his job. Maybe he pinned the mall robbery on me to get even."

Novak pointed the end of his pen at Ed. "You're saying this former mall Santa robbed the mall then tried to pin the whole thing on you so that he could get his job back?"

"It's a theory."

"A convoluted one." Novak shut his notebook. "I think you got it out for this guy."

"Why would you think that?"

"Because who would care enough about a mall Santa job to go through that much effort?

It's like a plot from a made-for-TV movie. No. Nobody would do that."

Ed shrugged. "I thought you might want to take a look at him, is all."

"Sure, you did. But I'll tell you what. I'll run this Malone through the system to see if it sounds like a personal vendetta. Call it a professional courtesy seeing as how we keep bumping into each other."

"Thank you."

"You got anything else about what happened tonight?"

Ed held up his burrito. "I still need to pay for this."

Novak motioned him inside. "Help yourself."

"That's how it usually is."

***

"Hey, Big Time," Nathan slid the burrito across the counter to read the price tag. "That was wild, wasn't it?" The clerk spoke rapidly, and his hands shook slightly.

Ed had been through enough high-stress incidents to know that people reacted to them differently. He guessed that Nathan was still dealing with the aftereffects of adrenaline and fear.

The store was silent now. No country-rap songs played from the store's radio.

Ed said, "Santa must have gotten the drop on you."

Nathan nodded. "For real, though." The clerk

convulsed as he spoke as if he didn't have complete control of his fine motor skills. "I had my back to the counter, and when I turned around, the guy was there. All jolly and strapped like."

"I thought you were carrying."

Embarrassment washed over Nathan's face, and his eyes darted about the store. "I left my piece at home."

"You did?"

"You know how it is." More hand waving. "Sometimes, a man don't want to carry. I was in a pacifist mood today. The reason for the season and all."

"And that's the day Santa struck."

"I know, right?" Nathan announced a total for the burrito. "But if it was another day, man, he would have been in for it."

"Clack, clack," Ed said.

Nathan snapped his fingers then pointed at Ed. His chuckle sounded forced. "That's right. You know it."

"Santa doesn't know how lucky he was."

"For real, though. Fool would have got a round going out the door." Nathan pointed his sideways thumb and finger at the door. "Just like that."

Ed frowned. "You'd shoot a man in the back?"

"Hells yeah. Front or back, the points are the same."

"The cops might have something to say about that."

Nathan's face whitened, but he patted his

chest. "The game is the game, baby." He didn't sound convincing. "If I'm going to get a penalty for playing, I'll pay the price. By the way, did you know we have a special on those chips you like? I can go grab a bag if you want."

Ed glanced out the window and noticed Detective Novak watching him. He wanted to ask Nathan a couple more questions but didn't want to do so with the cop nearby. He could always stop in another night.

He grabbed his burrito, said his thanks, and left.

Chapter 12

Ed walked up the flight of stairs and entered his apartment. Travis ran to him.

"Relax, you." Ed pushed the cat away as it rubbed against his leg. "We have rules in this house."

The tom didn't listen and circled back for another rub. Ed ignored him this time and walked into the kitchen. He tossed the Big Time burrito onto the counter then set about picking up the various items that the cat had knocked over this evening—his alarm clock, his book, and a plant that he would later need to reset.

Travis chattered and turned in a small circle.

"Settle down," Ed said. "What did you do when someone broke into the place? Did you greet them with this much enthusiasm, too?"

The cat darted off into another room.

"Maniac," Ed muttered.

He walked over to the apartment door and reconsidered it. How *did* someone gain access? The unit was on the second floor, and the door didn't appear to be kicked in, so options for entry were limited. Either the person knew how to pick locks, already had a key, or broke in through the window located off the fire escape.

He checked the window now. He hadn't checked it earlier when the detective was here but was pretty sure no one had entered that way. It was locked before he left and remained locked now.

Although maybe someone could have jimmied the window open, climbed through, then locked it behind them. When the intruder exited the apartment, they left via the front door to disguise their mode of entry. That seemed like an overly complicated notion, but it was one he needed to consider. Ed was sure Detective Novak would ponder it.

When his cell phone rang, Ed froze. His gaze snapped to the pillow that covered it. Several more rings occurred before it fell silent.

He hadn't given the number to anyone. It was a burner he'd purchased after he'd arrived in Utopia, and it was a bit of a security blanket. His previous witness inspector didn't want him to have a cell phone, but Marshal Goodspeed thought differently. She said he could get one anywhere, so she had to trust him not to do something stupid with it. If he wanted a phone, he could have one, but he couldn't contact anyone from his past. Doing so, even for a momentary check-in, would put not only him in danger but also those he called. A burner would give him anonymity for only so long.

There were ways to track any phone, Goodspeed had told him, even a burner. He wasn't sure about that, but technology was never Ed's strong suit. He decided to heed the marshal's warning and not use it for frivolous things.

Ed flipped over the pillow and opened the

phone. The screen lit up with a missed call from a number he'd committed to memory. Why were they calling him? They never did such a thing.

The phone brightened as another call from the same number arrived. He answered it this time.

"Hello?" a woman said. "Ed Belmont?"

"That's right."

"Fantastic." She sounded relieved. "For a moment, I thought maybe I dialed the wrong number."

Ed pulled the phone from his head to recheck the number. It was the correct number.

"Mr. Belmont?"

"Yeah?"

"This is Amy with Psychic Outreach," she said. "You're probably confused by the call."

"You could say that."

"We're affiliated with Horoscope Hook-up."

Ed grunted. The US Marshals had an emergency hotline set up for him to call. Previously it had been a travel agency, but that was burned when he told a civilian about it during an emergency. The marshals immediately changed it to Horoscope Hook-up. They must have created the Psychic Outreach department to communicate with him. However, it seemed an elaborate ruse when someone could have just called from Horoscope Hook-up for a customer satisfaction survey.

Amy continued. "Anyway, while doing an unrelated reading, one of our seers sensed trouble in your life. This was quite remarkable and caused our psychic deep concern. Of course, they asked that we reach out with a call. You're one of our best customers, and we wouldn't want anything to happen to you."

Someone somewhere in the marshal's office must have received a red flag warning that the cops recently ran Ed's name through the system. But that still didn't explain one thing.

Ed asked, "How did you get this number?"

Amy laughed. "We're psychics, Mr. Belmont. It's what we do. You should know that."

So, Marshal Goodspeed had been right. They had ways to track if he had a burner phone. Perhaps it was as easy as breaking into his apartment and manually checking. Someone else had already broken in to leave the Santa suit, so it must not be that hard. Or maybe the marshals did have some mind-bending technology that allowed them to spy on him.

Either way, Ed didn't like it.

"You're a psychic?" he asked.

"Not me."

"That's good because you don't want to know what I'm thinking right now."

Amy's tone turned serious. "If you like, you can talk with my supervisor."

"Is she a grumpy chain smoker?"

"No. Why do you think our psychic was concerned? You sound fine. Are you fine?"

"I'm fine."

From the other end of the line, there was clicking on a keyboard now. "So, Mr. Belmont, there were no recent problems that put you in contact with the local law enforcement community? Our seer was very specific in what they saw.”

Ed shrugged even though the caller couldn’t see it. “I had a conversation with a couple cops. Everything is working out fine.”

“So, it’s still in progress?”

“*Worked* out fine,” he corrected.

“Uh-huh,” Amy said. “Would you like one of our clairvoyants to come out and sit with you? Maybe they can help fix whatever problem you have found yourself in.”

“No.”

“Are you sure?”

“I’m sure.”

“Let me check on something.” More keyboard clicking now. “Yes, I see it right here. We have a grumpy chain smoker available. You seem to like that type.”

“I said I was fine.”

“She could be out in a day or so.”

“No.”

“You don’t have to be so snippy about it.”

“I’m not snippy.” Ed didn’t think he’d ever been snippy in his life. Rude and abrupt, sure, but never snippy.

“Let me assure you that it’s no trouble to send her out.”

He inhaled deeply and told himself to be calm. Very deliberately, he said, “I’ve got this. I can handle it.”

“So, it is still in process.”

Ed clenched his free hand into a fist. “No. It’s

been handled. It's done. Everything is fine."

"Okay."

"Besides, it's almost Christmas."

Amy said, "What's that got to do with anything?"

"I'm already meeting with your—what did you call the grumpy chain smoker?"

"A clairvoyant."

"I'm meeting with your clairvoyant after Christmas."

There was rapid-fire clicking on the keyboard now. "Oh, I see that right here. Yep. She'll help you see your future after that, I guess."

"I'm sure. She's a downright fortune teller that one."

Amy laughed. "That's her gift. You sure are lucky to have her."

Ed didn't think so.

"While you're on the phone, would you like me to read your horoscope?"

"Not really."

"It's no problem. Let's see." Amy tapped on her keyboard. "It says to avoid unexpected—"

He hung up on her.

Chapter 13

Yesterday's Books smelled like its namesake. Before his current lot in life, Ed Belmont might not have thought twice about this aroma. Now, the musty scent held promises of untold adventures.

He'd finished his latest novel a couple of evenings ago, but due to the previous day's excitement, Ed wasn't able to get a replacement book. He spent the previous evening rereading passages from the novel he'd just finished. It left him antsy for a new book.

Ed was on his way to the mall for another shift when he noticed Sorrell Babin inside the bookstore. The business wasn't open, but Ed tapped on the glass to get the owner's attention. Yesterday's Books wasn't scheduled to open for a couple more hours.

After Ed explained his situation, the older man let him inside.

"My business is too small to turn away a sale," Sorrell said. "And a man who carries his lunch to work should not be without a book."

Ed had to hurry, but he didn't want to make a wrong choice on his next book. Should he read another Parker novel, return to the Travis McGee series, or try something completely different? He decided to spend a few minutes perusing before selecting. He could afford to dawdle a little, even if it meant he had to hurry to make it to the mall. Usually, he gave himself plenty of time to get to work. Right now, that was something Ed had plenty of—time.

Ed didn't know anything about the books he scanned because the authors' names were still so new to him, but he knew he wanted to stay in the mystery genre. He had no interest in romance or horror. And who the heck read westerns? Probably the same type of people who read war books.

He didn't miss the irony in his current situation. Here he was searching for a book when, just a couple months ago, he'd been assigned to run a mystery bookstore in Pleasant Valley, Maine. At the time, he bristled at the idea and almost refused to read anything. The marshals had given him the opportunity of a lifetime, but it took Daphne Winterbourne for him to see it. Unfortunately, his past reared its head, and he lost that opportunity and her along with it.

Sorrell approached him then. He wore the same corduroy pants and soft leather shoes he had on the other day, but he had donned a new sweater today. The older man looked up from his hunched position. "Have you found anything yet?"

"I'm thinking about another Parker novel."

Sorrell touched his arm. "Parker is a fine read. He is one of my favorites, but he is a bad man. There are better men and women to read about."

"But I liked him."

"What did you like about him?"

"That he was a crook."

The bookstore owner rubbed his chin. "A crook, huh? Well, there are plenty of mystery-solving crooks to read about who are nicer than Parker."

"Who do you recommend?"

Sorrell wandered to the end of the mystery section and squatted. "Only got one of his in the store. He goes fast, so I am always on the lookout for more."

Ed took the book offered him. It was Donald Westlake's *The Hot Rock*.

Sorrell tapped the paperback. "This is about Dortmunder. Well, Dortmunder and his friends. There is a whole series about him. He is much nicer than Parker. About as lucky, though."

Ed truly liked Parker. More than that, he understood the man. He didn't know if he would like a nice crook.

"Funny fact," Sorrell said and pointed at the author's name on the paperback. "Westlake is Stark."

Ed cocked his head.

"Westlake wanted to write a darker character—Parker—but it was such a departure from his normal fare, he was afraid his fans would not like it. So, Westlake wrote under an assumed name."

"Stark."

Sorrell nodded. "That is right. For a time, the Parker novels were more successful than

Westlake's other books, including Dortmunder. But I have always liked the lighter fare. Parker is a bad man living a bad life. It's exceptional writing, but Parker is still a terrible person."

"But you don't think that's the same for this Dortmunder guy?"

"Dortmunder is funny and unlucky. He does not use violence the way Parker does. Violence is never the answer."

Ed knew that not to be true. Sometimes violence was a terrific answer. He turned the paperback over. Parker struck a chord in him the way that McGee hadn't. McGee made him want to be a better guy. Parker reminded him of who he was. He wasn't sure about this Dortmunder guy. And if Westlake had to change his name because he worried his fans wouldn't like it, what did that say about Dortmunder?

"Try it," Sorrell said. "No charge. If you like it, you come back and pay for it."

"How can a guy say no to that?"

Sorrell smiled and headed toward the counter.

"Hey, Sorrell?"

The older man stopped and turned.

"Who rented the apartment before me?"

"Why?"

"I'm wondering if the renter might still have a key."

Sorrell shook his head. "It is unlikely. He died."

Ed grunted in dismay.

"But do not worry; he did not expire in the

apartment."

Death didn't bother Ed. "How long did he live there?"

"Thirty-odd years. He was a little older than I am now. He was a nice man, but his taste in books was terrible. He loved the westerns. Why do you ask about a key?"

"I'm trying to figure out who broke into my apartment."

Sorrell's eyes widened. "Ah!" Now, a smile arrived on his lips. "You are an amateur detective, the best of all detectives."

"I don't know about that. I'm only trying to figure out who put the frame on me."

The older man excitedly touched the tips of his fingers together. "That is what a detective would do—*should* do. Let us think." Now, he rubbed his chin as a soft purring sound emitted from his chest. "I changed the locks before renting it to you so no one else would have a key."

Ed's brow furrowed. "That means they got in by picking the lock or coming in through the window on the fire escape."

Sorrell pointed. "Yes. That seems to be the only way."

"But why frame me?"

"How are they framing you?"

"Whoever broke into my apartment left behind a Santa suit and some money from the mall's robbery."

The store owner rubbed his chin again, and the purring sound returned. He seemed lost in thought for a moment. "It was not personal. You are new in town and the mall Santa Claus. The thief who did this is only trying to cast aspersions upon you to distract the police from looking at them."

Ed tapped the paperback against his open palm. "But the suit didn't fit."

"Uh-huh. Uh-huh. Maybe they did not consider that. Or perhaps they did but had no way to judge if it was the correct size. Or maybe they did not think you would put it on."

"If that's the case, they were amateurs." But then Ed considered the point of entry. "Picking a lock isn't easy. It's not like the movies."

"I would imagine not," Sorrell said. "So, they had some skill at the art. Is that what you are thinking?"

He was now.

"Another avenue to consider is someone wanted to point the police at you."

"So, this was personal?"

Sorrell shrugged. "Perhaps."

Ed had argued that it wasn't personal to Hurley when they discussed the Santa robber's attack. Could the mall manager have been correct? Was he targeted because of personal reasons?

Sorrell asked, "Who has it out for you?"

"There's a guy I can think of, but would he go to the extreme of breaking into my apartment? And would he have the skill to do so? Let alone knowing where I live."

"Those are a lot of questions for you to

answer."

Ed's eyes narrowed. "I'll get the answers."

"But do not forget to consider those you do not know."

"Huh?"

"Do not forget the people who would cast aspersions on you simply because you are the mall Santa Claus."

"How can I consider them if I don't know them?"

Sorrell rubbed his chin. He didn't purr this time. "I am stumped."

Ed smiled. "That makes two of us."

"I will tell you this," the store owner said, "right now is the perfect time to commit a crime as Santa."

"Because of the convenience store robber."

Sorrell nodded. "That man has already caused a stir. If someone were to commit another crime dressed as Santa, it would likely get lumped among the convenience store robberies."

"It does present a perfect opportunity."

The store owner tapped *The Hot Rock*. "It is something Dortmunder or Parker might do."

Ed considered it. "And dropping a Santa suit in my apartment for the cops to find would buy them more breathing room. It would help the police focus on me so they could commit more crimes."

Sorrell nodded. "Or make an escape."

"But the cops would have proved it wasn't me sooner or later. They found out I wasn't the convenience store robber last night."

Sorrell headed toward the cash register. "Then maybe it was only to harass you."

"Tis the season," Ed muttered.

***

The group of mall walkers hurried by the entrance as Ed Belmont stepped inside the Superior Mall. He watched them pass then turned in the opposite direction. He almost bumped into Arlo.

"Whatcha got there?" the older man asked.

Ed held up his lunch and *The Hot Rock*.

The older man's *US Air Force* hat sat pushed back on his head. His white t-shirt featured a talking gecko from an insurance company, and his sweatpants this morning were pink.

"I like your pants," Ed said.

Arlo swatted his hand in the air. "They belong to the wife. I spilled egg yolk on mine before leaving. I was fine going the way I was, but she wouldn't let me out of the house."

"So, you wore hers?"

"Who's gonna make any noise about what I'm wearing? You?"

Ed shook his head. "Not me. I think you look pretty."

"I know when you're putting me on."

"Any new excitement today?"

The older man looked down the hallway. "There was some dust-up between Eileen and the mall manager. He's a real jerk." Arlo made a fist. "I'd like to punch him right in the kisser."

"What was the argument about?"

"I don't know, but it happened right outside that store that used to sell snow boots and stuff."

"What do they sell now?"

Arlo frowned. "Nothing. Didn't you hear what I said? They used to sell them, and now they don't. It's empty. Kaput."

Ed shook his head. "I don't know which store you're talking about."

Arlo looked down the hall in the direction the mall walkers had gone. "They're gonna be a while. I can show you if you want."

"Lead on."

The older man headed away. "Keep up if you can."

Ed started to follow but stopped when he saw the word written across the backside of Arlo's sweats. "Juicy?"

"Shut up," Arlo said over his shoulder. "I already told you they're not mine."

"But they look good on you."

The older man stopped and faced Ed. He seemed about to say something mean but then reconsidered. A smile crossed his face. "Thank you."

Arlo spun on his heel and headed off. Ed dropped in behind him.

Chapter 14

"I want a pony," Lauren said.

Ed stared at the little dark-haired girl sitting on his knee. She wore a long red coat, white leggings, and black boots. He estimated her to be four years old.

"A pony?"

"A really big one."

"So, you want a horse?"

The little girl laughed. "A pony!"

"Uh-huh." He nodded and looked up. Susan Roskam was behind the camera. It appeared that she was having a tough time getting a photograph. Her face pinched as she jiggled the camera.

In the waiting line were seven kids. That wasn't too bad, but it was still early. The line would surely get longer as the day went on. With children around, things could always get worse.

From overhead, "Santa Claus is Coming to Town" played throughout the mall.

Ed eyed the little girl. "Anything else?"

"A pony as big as this." She lifted her hand high above her head. She strained to get it higher and almost slid off Ed's knee. He caught her and moved her back into position. Lauren said, "Bigger than my dog, Oscar."

Susan's face relaxed now as it appeared the camera might be working again. He'd only have to keep the little girl talking for a couple more minutes.

Ed glanced over to Lauren's parents. They were about the same age as him and stood arm-in-arm. The two looked like they were in an advertisement for some winter fashion promotion. Their clothes appeared new and were vibrant colors. They smiled brightly as if the little girl on his knee was the center of their world. Because of that, Ed imagined them to be boring conversationalists.

His gaze returned to the kid. "What kind of dog do you have?"

"He's a Great Dame."

"Dane."

Her head bobbed. "Uh-huh. And I want him to fetch like Oscar." She mimed throwing a stick.

"Ponies don't fetch."

Lauren met his eyes. "The one you bring me will. He'll be a magical fetching pony!"

"I'm not sure that will fit in my sleigh." He hoped no one he knew ever heard those words come out of his mouth. Maybe his dinner conversation would be on par with Lauren's parents.

The kid laughed. "Have my pony pull your sleigh with the other reindeers."

"Ponies don't fly either."

"Mine will."

"Right," Ed said. "Because it's magical."

Lauren giggled as she pushed her hand out into the air. "Swoosh!"

"A magical flying pony that fetches."

"That I'll name Riley."

"You want a unicorn."

"No." Lauren shook her head. "They have a horn on their head, and that's weird." She put her hand against her forehead and stuck her pinkie out. She wiggled the finger at him. "Don't you think it's weird, Santa?"

He did. He thought the kid was weird, too.

"Got it!" Susan called out. From behind the camera, she raised a thumb into the air.

Ed lifted the girl from his knee and set her on the ground. "A magical flying pony," he announced.

"That fetches!" Lauren shouted as she ran by Susan.

Lauren's parents eyed Ed with apparent confusion. The parents waiting in line all seemed distraught, but sudden excitement built within the children. Magical flying ponies that fetched were now in play for the holiday.

Susan approached Ed. She wore a headband with two snowmen bouncing atop their individual springs. Her sweater featured a giant gingerbread man. "Sorry about that."

"What happened?"

"I accidentally reset it to default. I've never done that before. It took me a minute to get it back the way I like it."

"Could someone else have done that to the camera?"

Susan cocked her head. "No. It was locked up in the mall office. Besides, who would mess with my camera?"

"Hurley would."

"He wouldn't. He's a lot of things, but a camera tweaker isn't one of them. And what would he get out of changing the settings?"

"I don't know. Maybe it was Raleigh."

That gave her pause, but she quickly shook her head. "No. That was all on me. I messed it up. My head's not in the game this morning."

Now that she mentioned it, Ed realized she hadn't called out Merry Christmas once today. That was very unlike Susan.

He asked, "Everything okay?"

"It's this whole Chet thing. I couldn't sleep last night because of it. Couldn't eat breakfast either. It's got me befuddled, but I'll be fine in a bit."

"How long did you guys work together?"

Susan looked over her shoulder to the line of waiting families. "We should get the next kid."

Ed grunted. "They can wait for a minute."

"But we've got quite a few in line."

"Seven," Ed said, "and this will only take a minute."

She glanced back again. "I thought there were more."

"Only seven. Trust me."

Susan returned her gaze to Ed. "Yeah, okay. What was your question?"

"How long did you work with Chet?"

"A few years."

"And was he always as crazy as you described him?"

"It got worse the more he thought of himself as Santa. He even grew the beard and put on some weight. He went North Pole for the role."

"What does he do during the off-season?"

"He's a painter."

"Like an artist?"

"Like the kind of guy who will change the color of your house." She mimed the up and down motion of a paint roller.

"Do you think he knows how to pick a lock?"

Susan shrugged. "How would I know? Probably not, but people have a lot of hidden talents." She looked toward the line as another family moved toward the back. "We should get the next kid."

"Last question," Ed said.

"Make it quick. They're stacking up."

Ed eyed the line. Whether or not he took the next kid, there would always be another. That's how children were—like flies at a picnic.

"It's about Santa suits," Ed said. "Is there a specialty shop to get these from? Someplace local maybe?"

Susan's brow furrowed. "Like a Big and Tall Store for wannabe Santas?"

The way she asked the question immediately revealed the problem in Ed's question. He should have phrased it differently. "Obviously, it would be—"

She interrupted. "I mean, the year-round demand for Santa suits is huge, so why wouldn't this town have a store? Is that what you're asking."

"Okay, I get it. There wouldn't be one in Utopia—"

Susan butted in again. "Although, a store like that would allow Santa to keep up with annual changes in fashion. How cool would that be? You know, bell-bottom suits, skinny-legged suits, wide collars, thin collars. Just imagine what could be done—seeing as how Santa is so hip and all. Fashionably Modern Santa, we could call it."

He crossed his arms. "Are you done?"

"I guess so."

"I take it the suits are bought online."

Susan nodded. "Or at a costume store. And it's not like they go out of style. Occasionally, people dump them off at thrift stores."

"What you're saying is there is almost no way to track these down?"

"There's no Santa suit registry if that's what you're asking."

Ed frowned. "What got into your coffee this morning?"

Susan shrugged a single shoulder. "It's the lack of sleep and the fact I'm always looking over my shoulder for Chet."

"Don't worry about him. He's not going to bother you while I'm around."

She smiled. "I hadn't thought about that."

"Well, do."

Susan glanced toward the waiting line. "Are you ready for the next kid?"

"No." Ed eyed the line of children. "But is anyone ever ready?"

Marjorie Lewis stood at the head of the line. The teenager in the Penguins jersey stood next to her. While Marjorie sought to make eye contact with Ed, the kid's attention was focused on his telephone.

For the past half hour, Marjorie and the boy had moved steadily up the queue. Ed watched them as he took request after request from a multitude of children. Marjorie and the teen never spoke to each other the entire time they were in line.

And now they were next.

Marjorie wore pink leggings and white tennis shoes. Her white sweatshirt was cut wide at the neck and draped low to expose her left shoulder. On the front of the shirt were the words *Pet Shop Bays*. Underneath the logo was a coiffed Shih Tzu and the tag line *West End Curls*.

Susan Roskam stood next to Ed. "What do you want to do?"

"Who's the kid?"

"She said it's her nephew."

"He looks fifteen."

"At least."

Ed eyed her. "Isn't that a little old for Santa?"

"Maybe his parents never told him."

They both looked toward Marjorie, who smiled and waved back excitedly.

"She's already paid for the full picture package," Susan said. "She must love him."

Ed sighed. "As soon as this is finished, I want a break."

"There's a place in heaven for you, Ed." Susan motioned Marjorie and her nephew forward.

As the two women passed each other, they both icily said the other's name.

"Suzy."

"Marge."

Marjorie and the teen stopped in front of Ed.

"Hi, Santa," she said.

Ed studied the kid. "Who are you?"

The teenager's eyes narrowed. "What do you care?"

"It's how we normally do it."

"No. Not this time."

Ed leaned an elbow on the armrest of the throne. "Okay, fine. Why don't we skip sitting on my knee, and you just tell me what you want for Christmas?"

The teenager rolled his eyes. "This is weird." He extended his hand toward Marjorie. "Pay up."

Marjorie slipped a few folded bills into his hand, then smiled at Ed. "Just some family business."

"See ya," the kid said. He jogged away and hurdled the velvet rope.

From behind the camera, Susan popped up like a prairie dog. "What just happened?"

But Ed knew. He'd been ambushed.

Marjorie laughed. "Well, since I'm here."

When she tried to slide onto his knee, Ed pushed her away. Marjorie grabbed the back of the chair and an armrest and pulled herself back on.

"I've been a good girl, Santa!"

Ed pushed Marjorie's hip, and she was almost out of the chair when someone in line yelled, "Let her stay!"

"Yeah!" someone else yelled. "Let her stay."

In a desperate move, Marjorie lifted her legs up and over the far armrest. She threw her arms around Ed's shoulders and clamped his neck in a bear hug.

"Santa!" she squealed.

Ed scooted to the edge of the chair. If he had to lift Marjorie and toss her like a sack of potatoes, he would. He had no compunction against doing such a thing.

He stood and hefted Marjorie into the air.

"Santa!" Susan yelled. She waved her hands back and forth as if she were signaling a landing plane.

It was then that Ed noticed it. The crowd was calling out, "Let her stay! Let her stay!" Many people pumped their fists in rhythm with the chant.

Several shoppers stood along the velvet rope recording the moment with their cell phones.

Ed flopped back into his chair and let go of Marjorie. She relaxed her grip around his neck. She quickly shifted her position on his knee then straightened her hair.

The crowd erupted into a loud cheer.

Marjorie smiled and waved at them. When she finally faced Ed, she said, "I've been a good girl this year.”

“I don’t care,” he muttered.

“This got messed up.” she repositioned Ed’s hat. “Much better.”

“What do you want, Marjorie?”

She leaned toward Ed’s ear. “What do *you* think I want?”

“I’m not going out with you.”

Her face registered shock, and she pulled back. Marjorie turned toward the crowd. “Why Santa! I could never do that.”

Susan’s face reddened as the crowd laughed. More shoppers stood along the velvet rope to enjoy the spectacle.

Marjorie leaned back into Ed and whispered, “Unless I dressed up as Mrs. Claus. Then I’d totally be willing to go out with you.”

Ed shook his head. He’d known some weird ladies in his time, but this one might have taken the cake.

“But for right now,” Marjorie said, “I only want a picture with you.” She turned toward the camera and leaned her head on his shoulder. “Smile, Santa.”

Susan stood frozen behind the camera-mounted tripod as she watched Ed and Marjorie.

“That’s all you want?” Ed asked. “A picture?”

“To remember our time together.”

Through clenched teeth, Ed said, “Take the picture.”

Susan didn’t move, however. Instead, she stayed frozen behind the camera. Her face had darkened with anger.

Marjorie pointed toward the camera. "C'mon, Suzy, take the picture."

Without looking through the lens, Susan pressed the photograph button on the camera.

"Was it a good one?" Marjorie asked.

Susan lifted her thumb.

"But you didn't look."

Susan's shoulders slumped. "It's fine."

Marjorie slipped off Ed's lap and happily said, "See you in the breakroom, Ed." Then she hurried off.

The assembled crowd clapped their approval.

Susan walked over but kept her eyes on the departing Marjorie. "I had no idea she would do that."

"I need a break."

"Can it wait until lunch?" Susan glanced at the line. "They're really lining up now."

Ed stood. "There's eleven of them. They can wait."

"What do you want me to tell them?"

"Tell them whatever you want."

Susan nodded. "I'll tell them you had to go to the potty."

He growled but didn't stop walking.

"What? Kids will understand that. Everyone goes to the potty. Even Santa."

Chapter 15

Christmas was only a couple of days away, and the attention that the Santa suit garnered bordered on ridiculous. Eager children and their overly accommodating parents approached Ed like he was a rock star.

But that was a silly thought. A rock star wouldn't cruise the halls of the Superior Mall hidden behind the red suit and white beard of jolly ol' St. Nick.

Ed didn't want to go to the mall's breakroom where Marjorie Lewis might accost him again. In his previous life, Ed would have been flattered by her advances. More than that, he would have taken advantage of them. But he wanted to be a better man, and part of that was to stay true to his desire to see Daphne Winterbourne again.

"Santa! Oh, Santa!" a woman yelled from down the hall. She stood with her husband and their three children. The family waved wildly at Ed.

He lifted a hand in their direction but didn't bother to stop and talk. He kept walking. That didn't deter the family as they continued to smile and wave.

"We'll meet you down at center court," the woman hollered cheerfully.

Ed raised his hand again but didn't look back

at them. Making eye contact might encourage more interaction, and that was something he didn't want.

He wished he could yank the suit off for fifteen minutes and slip into anonymity. Just walk around the mall without the repeated glances and the silly waving. While he enjoyed the recent discovery of people smiling and acknowledging him courtesy of a new identity— that never happened while he was a member of the Satan's Dawgs—the open fawning due to his portrayal of Santa bothered Ed.

It wasn't because it was a lie. He told plenty of untruths while with the club. And it wasn't because of the costume. He had worn several disguises when the illegality of the moment required it.

Ed hadn't fully put his finger on why it bothered him, but he was starting to believe it was the suspension of belief needed for the myth to continue. Ed could never remember a time he believed in Santa. From his youngest days, he knew there wasn't. He couldn't remember when it occurred exactly, but his mother had told him there wasn't a Santa Claus. While all the other kids his age walked around blathering on about Christmas, he knew it all was a hoax. For his entire life, Ed never once enjoyed the holiday drivel.

His gaze drifted by another family that waved. He raised a hand in acknowledgment but didn't stop walking. How could these people purposefully delude not only themselves but their children?

Ahead, John Hurley stepped out of a vacant unit between Kitchen Stitches and Hair Today Gone Tomorrow. The mall manager quickly looked both ways. Upon noticing Ed, he stiffened. "What are you looking at?"

"Nothing," Ed said.

"Keep it that way."

Hurley turned to the vacant unit and slipped his key into the lock. The windows of the suite were blacked out. All the vacancies were treated this way. Susan had explained this was done to minimize the visual impact of the vacant units.

Ed backpedaled so he could keep his eyes on Hurley. The man's behavior interested him.

The manager noticed Ed watching him. "What now?"

"What were you doing in there?"

Hurley motioned toward the now-closed unit. "I check all the vacancies to make sure there are no leaks or other issues going on. Not that it's any of your business. What are you doing walking around? Shouldn't you have some brat on your knee?"

Ed stopped walking backward. "I needed a break."

"A break?" The mall manager reared back. "You work four weeks a year, and you need a break? Where do I sign on?"

"You couldn't handle it. How can I get a key to one of those vacant units?"

Hurley's face darkened. "Why?"

"So I can go in there and get some quiet time."

"We have a breakroom for that."

"Marjorie won't leave me alone."

Hurley approached him. "I told you not to fraternize with the store owners."

"It's her, not me."

"Go out to your car." Hurley pointed toward the parking lot.

"I don't have one."

"What kind of man doesn't have a car?"

Ed wanted to say, "The kind who could punch a hole in your chest," but instead, he simply shrugged.

"No one goes into the vacant units but me."

"Why's that?"

"Because I said so." Hurley stepped forward until he was chest to chest with Ed. "What more do you need to know?"

Ed looked down his nose at the mall manager. The hardest thing about being in the Witness Protection Program was avoiding the old habits in his life—like making an arrogant jerk eat his words.

"That's what I thought," Hurley said. "Now, get out of my way. I have some grown-up work to do."

Ed stayed where he was and forced Hurley to step around him. The mall manager stalked away.

***

"What do you want for Christmas?" Ed asked.

The little boy named Marcus rubbed his

hands back and forth. "Anything."

"Anything?"

"Uh-huh."

"How old are you?"

Marcus held up four fingers. "And a half."

"So, probably not a motorcycle?"

The little boy shook his head and grinned. "Nuh-uh."

Marcus' mother stood at the edge of the velvet rope. She was an attractive woman with ebony skin. Her eyes were soft as she smiled at her son.

"How about an airplane?"

The kid shook his head.

"Too big, huh?" Ed recalled a toy recommendation from Susan. "How about a Throw Throw Burrito game?"

Marcus crinkled his nose. "I don't like burritos. They make my tummy rumble."

Ed chuckled. "I understand, but we've got to come up with something for Santa to bring you. What about a football?"

When Ed looked up again, Detective Stewart Novak stood next to Marcus' mother. The two didn't seem to know each other. Novak jerked his head to the side.

Marcus looked up at Ed with wide eyes. "I don't like football either."

"Okay, kid. We'll figure this out. How would you like to sit in Santa's chair for a minute?"

The little boy nodded.

Ed lifted Marcus from his knee and shifted him into the middle of the throne. "Now, don't give away any presents while I'm gone. Understand?" Ed couldn't believe the words that continued to fall from his mouth.

From behind the camera, Susan popped up. "What's going on?"

Ed pointed at the detective as he stepped toward the velvet rope.

Novak nodded at Marcus' mother. "Excuse us, ma'am. I need to borrow the big guy for a moment." He motioned Ed further down the rope.

"I'm working," Ed said. "This better be good."

"You look natural as Santa. I'd never have guessed."

"What's with the sunshine?"

The detective eyed the line of kids with their parents. "Has it been this way all day?"

"Why? You interested in a career change?"

"Not me. I don't like kids, but you must."

Ed shrugged. "Kids are all right." His brow furrowed. It must be sitting so close to the big fake tree that caused the stupid things to continue to erupt from his mouth. Too many plastic chemicals were leaching into his brain.

"Got any of your own?"

Ed cocked his head. "You asking me on a date, Detective?"

"Nah. I just came to see you at work."

"Why?"

"To make sure you were here."

Ed put his hands on his hips. "What for? What happened?"

"About ten minutes ago, another convenience

store was hit." Novak said. "Instead of going there, I came straight here."

"Why do that?"

"To rule you out."

"I appreciate that."

Novak nodded. "You're welcome."

"So what you're saying is that you don't believe my innocence even though I was a witness at the Quik N Go robbery."

Novak shrugged. "What can I say? I'm a professional skeptic."

"What about the fundraiser's heist? Do you still think I'm involved with that even though you found the wrong-sized suit in my apartment?"

The detective inhaled deeply. "I have my doubts. I'll give you that much. But you'll remain in the keep-under-observation column until further notice."

"Good to know." Ed didn't like any cop keeping an eye on him, but he had to play it cool. "What's it going to take for you not to have any doubts?"

"We catch the guy who did it. When that happens, I'll stop having doubts about you."

Ed's gaze drifted back to Santa's throne. Marcus sat in the middle of the oversized chair. The young boy smiled broadly and waved at the other kids in line. "I need to get back."

"One other thing."

"What's that?"

"That tattoo." Novak pointed at his right hand even though it was in a glove. "You said you got that fifteen years ago.”

“I might have been mistaken.”

“Is that so? Well, a ball of fire on the back of a right hand comes up in some reports back west. A real bad character is associated with them.”

Ed shrugged. “It’s lucky I’m not him. I’ve never been arrested.”

“Just a couple of traffic tickets,” Novak said.

“You’ve been checking up on me, Detective.”

“It’s what I do.”

“A professional skeptic,” Ed said.

“Anyway, that tattoo got me thinking.”

“About?”

Now, it was the detective’s turn to shrug. “I don’t know. Just thinking in general.” Novak motioned toward Santa’s throne. “You better get back. That kid looks ready to take your job. I’ll be in touch.” He turned and walked away.

When Ed lifted Marcus from the chair, he said, “Have you figured out what you want for Christmas?”

The kid beamed. “I want to be Santa!”

“It’s not all it’s cracked up to be. Anything else?”

“I want to do this.” Marcus continued to wave and smile at the people in line.

He set Marcus on his feet, gave him a push toward Susan, then announced, “He wants a parade float.”

Chapter 16

After finishing his shift for the day, Ed changed back into his street clothes and packed his Santa suit into its large storage bag. He slipped his leather jacket on and closed the locker. Before heading home, he had one stop to make inside the mall.

"Santa Baby" played through the speakers overhead.

The security office was at the opposite end of the mall. Unlike the management office, this was in a more prominent location. Eileen Webster sat behind her desk and appeared to be completing some paperwork. A line of monitors on the west wall showed various sections of the mall's interior and exterior.

Eileen looked up when Ed stepped into the office. "Look what the cat dragged in."

"I came to see your camera system."

She set down her pen. "Took you long enough."

"Busy day."

"I saw. It's like a never-ending line of ankle-biters. So, what's the real reason you're here?" She leaned back and crossed her arms. "You want to make sure that assault on Chet didn't get recorded?"

"That's not it."

"Sure, it is. Trust but verify about the

recordings. Tell me I'm wrong."

He turned his palms upward.

"And here I thought you might want to do a little gossiping."

"I'm Santa. All the gossip I've got comes from kids."

"I could talk to my sister if I wanted that." Eileen stood and walked over to the wall of monitors. "See? The cameras are working fine."

Ed leaned in to view various portions of the mall as well as the exterior. Every few seconds, the cameras changed angles, and it was as if the whole wall rippled in motion. In the middle of the bottom row of monitors was a computer screen. It flashed an error message.

"This," Eileen said, tapping the screen, "is where everything would normally be saved. But something happened to the hard drive. At least, that's what I think happened." She jiggled the computer mouse, and a white cursor appeared. It hovered over a Record button. Eileen pressed the left button on the mouse, and an error message appeared on the screen—Unable to Record.

"D.O.A.," she said

"And the mall owners won't chip in and upgrade the system?"

"With what money?"

Shoppers walked by the security office with bags in their hands.

"It's a mall," Ed said. "The people who own it have to be rich, right?"

Eileen laughed. "Who knows how rich they

are? That's got nothing to do with nothing."

Ed furrowed his brow. "Sure, it does."

"Have you seen how many vacancies there are out there? Dozens." Eileen pushed her swivel chair back then walked over to the window to point into the hallway. Across the way were two empty spaces. "To those folks who own this joint, it's only about one thing. The Benjamins." She rubbed her thumb and fingers together. "Get it?"

Ed understood the concept of money. The Satan's Dawgs did many illegal and desperate things to make sure there was enough of it to go around.

Eileen continued. "A mall runs on rents, and when there isn't much coming in, the whole thing falls into disrepair. Or haven't you noticed?"

He'd seen the vacancies, but he hadn't noticed any physical issues with the malls.

"The parking lot is littered with potholes."

"I hadn't noticed."

"How could you not?"

Ed shrugged. "I don't have a car, plus there's snow."

"Take my word for it; it's bad. The mall has seen better days, and those were about twenty years ago." She squinted one eye and rolled the other toward the ceiling. "Maybe forty, but whatever it was, it was before our time."

Ed leaned toward the monitors again. "There are a lot of people shopping, though."

"Because it's Christmas. Don't let that fool

you. Most people buy their things online now. They only come in to get those items they can't get there, and one of those things is you."

He eyed Eileen.

"A kid can't virtually sit on Santa's lap. Well, maybe they can, but it's not the same. Know what I mean? You're an American institution, Ed. Like apple pie and baseball."

He tapped the monitor where a vacant unit was shown. "How often does Hurley walk through the empty units?"

Her expression darkened, and her thumb absently rubbed an empty spot on her belt. "He doesn't check the vacants."

"He said he did, and I saw him coming out of one near Hair Today Gone Tomorrow."

"Maybe he does now, but the security team did it before."

Ed faced Eileen. "What happened?"

She turned her attention toward the monitors again. "We walked through them every week, but we're shorthanded now, so he took the responsibility away."

"How many are on the security team now?"

"It's just me. Budget cuts, or so Hurley says."

Ed studied her. "A one-person security team for a mall of this size seems irresponsible."

"A mall of any size should have more than one person."

"Who handles the security when you're not here?"

"I'm here seven days a week right now. I'm getting paid overtime. The couple of hours in the morning when I'm not here, Hurley covers it."

Ed shook his head. "But wouldn't it be cheaper to just hire a second person and pay them minimum wage instead of paying you overtime?"

Eileen dropped back into her swivel chair. "I don't know what's going on with the ownership group's decision-making, but I'll tell you this much—after Christmas, I'm gone. I'm not hanging around here any longer."

"Got another job lined up?"

"I'll figure out something, but I can't keep this pace up. This ownership group isn't loyal to us, so why should we be loyal to them?"

Ed's gaze drifted back to the monitors. He noticed another empty suite on one of them. "So, only Hurley is checking the vacants now?"

"He told me to not worry about them until he gets another person hired. Like that's going to happen any time soon." Eileen's brow furrowed. "Why are you so interested?"

"I saw him coming out of one." He touched the monitor for the vacant suite next to Kitchen Stitches. "Got a key to go take a look?"

Eileen shook her head. "Hurley took them all."

"Even the duplicates?"

"What can I say? The man was thorough."

"How long ago did he take them?"

She rested her arms on the edge of her desk. "A few days ago."

"Right before the robbery."

Her eyes narrowed. "What are you getting at,

Ed?"

"I don't know. I'm just asking questions."

"That you are." Eileen faced the monitors and leaned into the one that flashed the vacant suite near Kitchen Stitches. She seemed about to say something but stopped herself. She abruptly turned back to Ed. "Anything else?"

"I'm good."

Eileen slid some paperwork back in front of her. "I'll see you tomorrow," she muttered as she checked off several boxes.

***

A country rap song played through the Quik N Go when Ed entered.

Behind the counter stood Nathan the clerk. A red bandanna was tied around his forehead. On top of that, his camouflaged baseball hat sat sideways on his head.

The pale man swung his hands from side to side as he rhymed along with the song. "Bust you in the mouth like a rainbow trout." He mimed throwing a wild punch. "Take you down south to remove all doubt."

Ed walked to the cooler and selected another Big Time Burrito. This would be his third night in a row. He should probably eat something different for his health, but no one was here to complain or chastise him. As he walked back toward the counter, he grabbed a bag of jalapeno chips.

Nathan stopped his rhyming and said, "Yo,

Big Time. How goes it? No traumatic disorder, I see." He pressed a couple of buttons on the cash register.

"From the burritos?"

The clerk's eyes widened. "Nah, man, the robbery. You was here when I got rolled." He slapped his hands against his chest. "That's like hazardous duty, know what I'm saying?"

Maybe it had been traumatic for Nathan, but Ed had been in far more dangerous situations. "You were scared?"

"Not me. No way." Nathan shook his head as he selected a couple more buttons on the register. "But I thought maybe you were. You know since you had to witness the whole thing. Must've been intimidating and all."

"Totally," Ed said. "Tell me something. How did Santa get the drop on you?"

Nathan rolled his eyes. "You know how it is. I'm over here just doing my thing—"

"Rapping and dancing?"

"Like I said—doing my thing—when I look up, and ol' Saint Nick himself is sticking a gat in my grill. He's lucky he caught me unawares, or I would've busted him in the mouth."

"Like a rainbow trout."

"Exactly!" Nathan mimed an uppercut. "Pow. That's how we do."

"Did you get a look at the mark on his wrist?"

"Yo, I did! You saw that, too?"

Ed nodded. "I only saw the mark, though. I was too far away to see what it was."

Nathan's eyes narrowed. "I'll tell you what.

Santa best pray for my forgiveness if he comes back in here because he ain't getting another crack at this register. It'll be shoot first and ho-ho-ho second." Nathan pantomimed a sideways gun. "Know what I'm saying?"

"What was it?"

The clerk looked at his extended thumb and fingers. "This is supposed to be my gun."

"Yeah, I get that. What was the mark on his wrist?"

"Right." The clerk covered his mouth. "Oh, snap. I forgot all about that. It was a tattoo of a bird with its wings out or something." Nathan spread his arms wide. "Like this."

"That's it."

"Yup." The clerk announced a total for the items. "A stupid thing to get on your arm if you ask me. Not at all cool like that one on your hand. That's like from a race car or something, right?"

Ed handed him several bills. "Nope."

The clerk absently took the money. "Then what is it?"

"A ball of fire."

"That's it? You don't got some story to go with it?"

Ed did, but he wasn't going to share it with Nathan.

As Nathan placed the bills into the register, he continued to talk. "My tattoos have reasons behind them." He pulled up a sleeve. "This one is the dude from *Gears of War*. Super tough character. Great game." He pointed to a company logo on the opposite arm. "Of course, you know what Mountain Dew is."

"I do."

Nathan grinned. "I got a Twinkie on my right calf and the McDonald's M on my shoulder."

"And those have meaning?"

"For real. Like I love those things." He put his hand over his heart. "They fulfill my life."

"Twinkies and Mountain Dew?"

Nathan nodded. "Don't forget the Big M." He hummed the McDonald's theme song.

"Did you tell the cops about the bird tattoo?"

Nathan cocked his head. "What bird tattoo?"

"On Santa's wrist."

The clerk chuckled. "That's right. A lot was going on, you know, and it sort of slipped my mind. You think I should call and tell them?"

Ed picked up the items. "It's up to you."

"Right," Nathan muttered. "Player play on and all that."

"Live and let live."

The clerk glanced toward the door. "But let that fool try to come back here."

Ed eyed Nathan. "I doubt he will, but if he does...."

"Yeah?"

"Keep that double-fingered gun holstered."

Ed was to the door before Nathan said, "I forgot my piece at home, yo!"

***

At his apartment, Ed quietly ate his burrito

while reading *The Hot Rock*. Nearby, Travis hovered over his food bowl and crunched on several kibbles.

Ed enjoyed the early portion of the Dortmunder novel, but his mind drifted away. At one time, he pondered the mall robbery.

If Dortmunder had been involved, how would he have set up the heist? Ed was too early in the book to know how the master criminal thought. What about Parker, then? Ed had read only one book of the man, and that was more of a revenge tale. He had no idea how Parker might plan the heist.

He smiled at the thoughts. Speculating how two fictional criminals might have pulled off a real-life heist was something Ed would never have done previously. This was all new behavior brought on by reading books. It was like imagining which superhero was tougher. That was a conversation Ed remembered having when he was very young—roughly four or five. Then that kind of silly fantasy was knocked out of his life by his mother.

Her life was a calamity wrapped in chaos, and it forced him to grow up quickly. Imagination and happiness were casualties of their home life. They'd get to come out when Ed visited his grandmother. As he grew, his childhood creativity died and was replaced by an ingenuity for criminal activity.

Ed's grin faded, and he bit into his burrito.

He didn't want to spend his time blaming his mother for how his life turned out. Things were his responsibility now. Where he went and how he acted were things he could control.

Briefly, he thought about picking up his phone and calling his grandmother. He didn't care about the upcoming holiday, but to hear her voice again would be fantastic. He knew he could never see her again. That would put her in too much danger. He shouldn't call her for the same reason.

The same thing went for Daphne Winterbourne. If he could just hear her voice...

Ed quickly pushed her from his mind. To linger on these thoughts was unnecessary, and they only added to the dismay he currently felt.

Ed's gaze returned to the page, and he struggled to push these thoughts from his mind.

Chapter 17

The door to the breakroom swung open, and Susan entered. "Hurley is late this morning."

Ed stopped buttoning his Santa jacket to study her. This morning, Susan wore a green sweater dress covered with garland and baubles. On top of her head, a single star bobbled at the end of a spring. She looked like a walking, talking Christmas tree.

"*What?*" she asked.

"Nothing."

Susan looked down at her sweater dress. "You don't like how I'm dressed?"

"It's not that. I haven't seen that outfit yet."

"It's new. Do you like it?"

He smoothed the front of the red jacket. "It's nice. What's this about Hurley?"

"He's usually here before us, so I like to check in with him." Susan pulled at the edges of her dress. "Now, you got me worried. Is it too much?"

"It's fine. Why do you want to check in with Hurley?"

"To play nice, I guess."

"Keep your friends close, but your enemies closer." Ed clicked his tongue against the back of his teeth. "A good philosophy, I guess."

Susan eyed him. "What happened in your childhood to make you so cynical?"

"Has he ever been late?"

"Not in the years I've known him. He's always been early. Maybe he's sick."

"If we could be so lucky."

She harrumphed. "That's terrible, Ed. And so close to Christmas."

As he slipped the white beard over his head, an idea came to him. "Is there anyone in his office?"

"Like who?" Susan tugged on Ed's beard to adjust it into place. "He let his assistant go earlier in the year due to budget cuts."

"So I've been told. Where's Raleigh?"

"I haven't seen him around either. He's probably fixing something with duct tape and baling wire."

Ed quickly fitted his wig into place before snatching his Santa hat from a locker.

"Wait," Susan said. "Your hair isn't right."

"I'll be back."

"You can't go out looking like that."

"I'm not going far." Ed stepped into the empty hallway.

"Where are you going? Some kids might see you."

The breakroom door closed behind him. He stepped over to the mall office and tried its doorknob. Locked.

Susan opened the breakroom and stuck her head out. "What are you doing? I told you Hurley hadn't come in yet."

Ed moved to the maintenance room.

"Now what?"

With a quick twist of the lock, he was inside.

"Ed, answer me," she said.

The door shut behind him but immediately reopened. Susan followed him in. "What the heck are you up to?"

The maintenance room was filled with shelves, workbenches, and cabinets. It smelled of grease and old metal objects. Leaning against a post was a hand truck with a missing wheel.

Ed searched the various countertops then the hooks on the walls. After that, he yanked open several drawers.

Susan followed him as he moved throughout the room. "Tell me what you're looking for?" she whispered.

"I'll know when I see it."

"Isn't that great?" She glanced back toward the door. "You're going to get us in trouble."

"Then step outside and keep watch."

"Why do I have to keep watch? I don't even know what you're looking for."

Ed had recently been a maintenance man in a retirement community. His supervisor there had a master key to most of the suites in the building. Ed was never given one because he was the new guy.

"You're starting to act like Chet."

He ignored the slight and kept pulling open drawers. It seemed unlikely that Ed would find a key in the lower ones, but he checked them, nonetheless. He tugged on the last drawer. Inside was a half-empty bottle of whiskey.

Susan blocked his path now. "Tell me what

we're doing."

"I'm looking for a master key."

Her eyes widened. "Why?"

"To get into the mall office."

"What do you want to find in there?"

Ed looked at her.

"You'll know it when you see it." Susan smirked. "Right."

He closed the drawer and straightened. There were no keys to be found.

"You want to break into Hurley's office to look for something you don't know about. Why don't I believe you?"

"Something doesn't make sense," Ed said.

"Exactly. You're not telling me why you want to break into Hurley's office."

He waved her off. "Hurley's got no help. The security staff is down to one person, and they won't fix the camera system so that it actually functions."

"Why do you care?"

Ed searched another counter. "And there's only one maintenance guy, who spends half his time hiding out from real work. How are they keeping this place operational?"

Susan shrugged.

"You already said it—with duct tape and baling wire. This whole place is not right, and I want to know why."

"You're Santa," she whispered, "not Sherlock Holmes. Don't stick your nose where it doesn't belong."

"Travis McGee would stick his nose where it

didn't belong."

"Who?"

Ed pulled open a drawer—no keys. "He's a protagonist who often finds himself in complicated mysteries and unfortunate situations."

Susan made a funny face. "Okay, nerd, did you get a thesaurus for Christmas or something?"

He straightened. "Nerd?"

She rolled her eyes. "Protagonist?"

"It's the star of a book."

"I know what it is. Can we do this book club somewhere we won't get in trouble?" She motioned toward the door. "Let's get out of here."

"Just because I read doesn't make me a nerd."

"Don't get your panties in a bunch. Let's go. I don't want us to get kicked out of the mall. This is my job. Yours, too."

Ed frowned. "My panties aren't in a bunch."

The door to the maintenance room opened, and Raleigh stepped inside. "Hey! What're you two doing in here?"

"Hi, Raleigh," Susan said. "Good to see you." She chuckled nervously. "What are you doing here?"

While Susan's reaction to the moment was to be cheerful, Ed's was to stare silently.

"This is my shop," Raleigh said. "And don't 'hi' me. What are you doing here?" He stepped forward, but he stopped. His gaze swept over the basement. "Did you touch my stuff?"

"We were looking for a screwdriver," Ed said.

Raleigh faced him now. "For what?"

"The left arm on the throne wobbles a bit." Ed jerked his left hand back and forth for show. "I wanted to tighten it."

Raleigh tapped his chest. "I do that."

"I didn't want to bother you."

"It's my job. These are my tools."

"Yeah," Ed said. "No problem."

Raleigh moved toward a counter and selected a couple of screwdrivers. "I'll fix it for you now. That's what I do. You shoulda asked me."

Ed eyed the ring of keys attached to Raleigh's belt. There was probably a master key on there. He could risk asking the maintenance man to let him into the manager's office, but Raleigh might be loyal to Hurley. Besides, any story he told to gain access might come back to haunt him later if Raleigh let it slip. It was a better plan to let it lay for the moment and worry about access later.

But maybe he could ask Raleigh to let him into the vacant units—especially the one next to Hair Today Gone Tomorrow. Doing so, however, might come back to bite him, just like asking to go into Hurley's office.

"Anything else?" Raleigh asked.

Ed eyed Susan then shook his head. "Just the screwdriver."

"Good." Raleigh pointed at the door. "Then get out."

***

"What do you want for Christmas, Asher?"

The boy stared up at him. This kid didn't have the wide-eyed fascination that most of the other kids had. Instead, he had a steely calmness that seemed unnatural for a child his age. Ed estimated him to be about five.

Overhead, "I Saw Mommy Kissing Santa Claus" played throughout the mall. Shoppers walked by, and the din of activity seemed higher than usual. The excitement of Christmas being only a couple of days away had finally arrived.

"You're not Santa." Asher stated this with complete conviction. Gone was the natural uncertainty of a child.

Ed smiled. "Sure, I'm Santa."

The boy shook his head. "I saw another Santa on the news."

"The one robbing the stores? He's an impostor. Do you know what that is?"

Asher nodded. "It's make-believe. What about the Santa at the grocery store? The one who rings the bell? Is he an impostor, too?"

Ed nodded and felt silly for doing so. He didn't even like kids, but now he was doing his best to further the lie of Old Man Christmas. He'd become part of the machine—a simple cog—that tries to separate people from their hard-earned money and brainwash a generation of children. Even though he knew that, the emotionless boy on his knee bothered him. The kid should be excited about the impending holiday.

From behind the camera, Susan Roskam lifted her hands and shrugged.

Ed touched the boy's back. "Smile at the camera, Asher."

The boy forced a lopsided grin, and Susan soon lifted her thumb into the air.

"Got it," she called. "It's not great, but I got it."

Asher faced him again. "How come they're impostors, and you're not? The real Santa lives in the North Pole. You live here with us."

"I'm real," Ed said. "You're sitting here with me."

"Where are your reindeer? Where are your elves?"

Against his better judgment, Ed liked this kid and wanted him to at least smile a little. "If you don't believe I'm Santa, why are you here?"

Asher glanced toward a young couple standing at the velvet ropes. The man had his arm around the woman. The woman beamed with pride, but the man appeared to be deeply concerned. They were dressed in worn jeans, and their winter coats appeared to have been through several seasons.

"My dad wants me to believe in Santa," Asher said.

"What about your mom?"

"Her, too."

Both parents waved at the boy. As the father shook his hand in the air, his jacket slid down his arm and exposed a mark on his wrist. It no longer looked like a greasy smudge to Ed. From where he sat, he could clearly see the tattoo.

He leaned toward Asher. "Why does your dad want you to believe?"

"Because he lost his job."

"And your mom?"

"She's still working."

Susan made a circling motion with her hand then eyed the line of eight waiting kids.

"Dad told Mom that Santa would make everything right this year. We just have to believe."

Ed leaned back in his chair.

"Santa?" Asher asked.

"Huh?"

"I don't want anything for Christmas."

"You've been a good boy, haven't you?" Ed didn't feel foolish asking this question, and he didn't care who heard it.

Asher nodded.

"So, what do you want?"

"For my dad to get a new job."

Ed studied the father. "How about I bring you a football?"

Disappointment spread across Asher's face. "Yeah, I guess."

He lifted the boy from his knee and set him on the ground. "A football," Ed announced without any enthusiasm.

Asher shuffled toward his parents. When he arrived, the parents wrapped their arms around his shoulders and left.

Susan walked over. "Ready for the next one?"

"Did you get the names of those parents?"

"Naturally. They bought a picture. Why?"

***

After a couple of hours, Ed and Susan took a walk. Those in line groaned when they announced that they would be right back, but Ed needed to stretch his legs. Sitting for hours with a steady line of children on his knee might not be the worst thing he could imagine in his life, but he would have to make sure to thank Marshal Goodspeed the next time he saw her.

When they walked past a vacant suite, Ed asked, "What do you think about Raleigh?"

"I try not to."

"Is he loyal to Hurley?"

She shrugged. "Why do you ask?"

"I want to ask about those keys he's got."

"What for?"

Ed motioned toward an empty suite. "I want to look in a couple of these vacants."

"I thought you wanted to check out Hurley's office."

"That, too."

"What's gotten into you?"

"I'm trying to put together some pieces of a puzzle."

"What puzzle?" Susan stopped walking. Ed took a couple more steps then stopped as well. He turned to face her.

"What?" he asked.

"Are you playing detective?"

"No."

"It seems like it." Susan moved forward and stood directly in front of Ed. "You're asking questions about Hurley and Raleigh. And what about that family from earlier? You wanted their information. Tell me why you wanted that."

"That's unrelated."

"I don't care. Tell me."

"It was something their kid said. It made me feel bad."

"*You* felt bad?" Susan touched his arm. "What did he say?"

"That his father was out of work."

Her look was incredulous. "This is Utopia. Take a look around. We've got rampant unemployment here since the factories shut down. I bet every other kid on your knee has a father out of work. Do you want their addresses, too?"

Ed looked away.

"You're not the real Santa."

"I know that."

"Don't turn into Chet."

His eyes snapped back to her. "I'm not."

"Then what's with this detective thing?"

"Who said I'm doing that?"

She cocked her head. "You did, Mr. Travis McPhee."

"McGee."

"Whatever. You want to investigate places you have no business being. Listen, Ed. My whole business relies on you. If you screw up, it reflects on me. If you do something stupid, I'm out my livelihood."

Ed gently touched her upper arm. "I'm not doing anything that will get either of us in trouble."

"Why are you doing anything at all?"

Ed wanted to tell her about his time with the Satan's Dawgs. That as the club's bookkeeper, he was assigned to resolve challenging tasks for the club. It was a responsibility he took seriously—deadly serious. And it was hard to let that type of responsibility go. When things were wrong, he wanted to get involved somehow—to fix them in a way that made things okay again.

The fact that someone robbed the mall didn't bother him. It also didn't bother him that someone was robbing convenience stores. Things happened in life that were neither good nor bad. What bothered him was that someone tried to frame him, which dragged him into the whole mess.

Had they left him alone, Ed wouldn't have cared who robbed what, but he couldn't tell Susan all of that. She stared at him expectantly. He had to tell her something.

"Someone planted a Santa suit in my apartment," Ed said.

"I know that."

"They also dropped a single jug full of money."

"I know that, too. The cops already cleared you of that."

Ed shrugged. "I want to know why someone did that to me and, if possible, I want to exact a little payback."

Her eyes narrowed. "Payback? What kind of payback are you talking about?"

"To have them arrested. What other kind of payback is there?"

Susan exhaled. "For a second there, I thought you might do something violent."

Ed spread his arms wide. "I'm Santa. Is Santa a violent man?"

"You punched Chet while wearing that suit."

"Yeah, but that was different," Ed said. "He had it coming."

Susan smiled. "Still."

Chapter 18

"It's a what?" Ed asked.

"A Bubble Machine Gun." The little girl named Amanda positioned her hands as if she were holding a rifle. "The pink one."

"And it makes bubbles?"

She nodded once, very emphatically. "Lots of them."

"Why do you want it?"

Amanda laughed and threw her hands in the air. "Because it makes bubbles!"

"Of course." He lifted the girl from his knee and put her on the ground. "A Bubble Machine Gun," he announced.

The girl cheered and ran toward her waiting parents.

Susan, on the other hand, appeared upset. She quickly approached. "You can't say that."

"What?"

"Gun," she whispered, then glanced around. "Let alone machine gun. We don't condone that type of thing."

Ed didn't care about guns. He didn't have a silly love affair with them like some members of the Dawgs. To him, they were simply tools—like a hammer or an ax. The mere mention of a gun seemed about as scary as saying shovel. "I don't see the problem."

"It's part of our creed," Susan whispered.

"Didn't we go over this?"

They probably did, but she had so many rules to being Santa that Ed had tuned many of them out.

"Never suggest a toy that is a gun, a knife, or a weapon of any kind. You remember?"

"No."

She put her hands on her hips. "Well, now you know."

Ed glanced at the line of kids—nine. "We're two days from Christmas. I did pretty good up until now."

"You got lucky."

"Maybe kids don't care about guns anymore."

"You'll see," Susan said. "You tell one of them they can have a rattlesnake, then they'll all want a rattlesnake."

"Take it easy. It's a plastic toy that blows bubbles. Not a rattlesnake."

Susan pointed at him. "No more guns. Got it?"

Without waiting for a response, she left to get the next kid.

"Yeah," he muttered under his breath. "I got it. No more fun stuff."

Ed looked down the hall. In front of one of the vacant suites, John Hurley appeared to berate Raleigh Dunham. The maintenance man hung his head as the manager leaned into him. Raleigh removed the key ring from his belt and dropped it into Hurley's open hand. The two men parted after that.

"Santa, this is Gianna."

Ed turned to find Susan standing with a small girl with a wide grin. "I want a Bubble Machine Gun, too!"

Susan raised her eyebrows. "Told you."

***

"Do you hate me?" Marjorie Lewis asked.

Ed bit into his sandwich and chewed.

They were in the mall's breakroom. The chair holding Santa's jacket, hat, and beard sat between them.

"Come on, Ed. Answer me."

He swallowed, feigned like he was about to answer, then took another bite of the sandwich.

Marjorie said, "How rude," then dropped her chin onto her palm. Her elbow rested on the breakroom's table. "I can do this all day."

Through a mouthful, he said, "I'm only here for my lunch."

"Well then, I can do this for your whole lunch."

"Help yourself."

Marjorie clucked. "I will."

She wore a denim mini skirt with two thin belts and ankle-high boots. Her t-shirt read *The World is Going to the Dogs.* Several colorful bracelets gathered around her right wrist.

Marjorie shifted in her seat. "How come you don't pay attention to me?"

"I already got a girl."

Even though Ed and Daphne Winterbourne had never been an item, he wanted to remain true to her. Besides, it felt good to think of her as his girl.

Marjorie stiffened. "What girl? You mean Susan?"

"You don't know her."

"Right." She nodded knowingly. "And she's probably from New York. As if I haven't heard that before."

"Maine," he said. Ed didn't see any harm in saying where Daphne lived.

Marjorie's chin returned to her open palm. "This girl doesn't even live close by?"

Okay, maybe there was some harm in admitting it.

"Why's she not here with you?" Marjorie asked.

"It's complicated."

She canted her head. "Is it complicated because of her or complicated because of you?"

Ed bit into his sandwich. He had already said too much, and he needed to stop talking.

"If it's complicated because of her, then why are you torturing yourself? Move on. And if it's complicated because of you—" Marjorie's eyes narrowed. "Then that makes you even more interesting. What's going on inside that head of yours? Inquiring minds want to know."

"What do you know about Raleigh?"

Marjorie's face hardened. "Why? What did Susan say?"

Ed lowered his sandwich. "She didn't say anything."

"She said something." Marjorie's shoulders

slumped, and she looked away. "She promised not to."

"I don't know what you're talking about."

"We went out once."

"You and Raleigh?"

She lowered her eyes. "Okay, maybe it was twice." Marjorie faced him fully now. "But it was no more than that. You gotta believe me."

Ed shrugged. "Whatever. It doesn't concern me."

"But you just asked about him."

"I changed my mind."

Marjorie leaned forward. "You don't know how hard it is to meet people when you're a small business owner inside the mall. The hours I work are insane, and I don't have a life of my own. The only people I talk to all day are dogs and cats. They're great and all, but you get my point."

Ed stared at his sandwich. This wasn't the kind of information he wanted. He pulled the two pieces of bread apart for no other reason than to remain distracted. Inside was still peanut butter and jelly. He closed the sandwich but didn't bother looking up.

"So," Marjorie said, "I went out with Raleigh one time. Big deal."

"Twice," Ed muttered.

"But that was it. I promise. And nothing happened." She rolled her eyes. "All right. He might have kissed me, but that's where it ended. So that you know."

Ed studied the opposite side of the sandwich

now. It appeared the same as the other. He still didn't bother looking up.

"So what if he took me to the Sizzler both times before it closed down? It's not like others haven't gone there."

Ed reopened his sandwich. It could use more peanut butter, he decided.

"Anyway," Marjorie said, "I took that as a sign. The closing, not the Sizzler. Well, okay, maybe there were more signs than just that. It's Raleigh we're talking about after all."

Ed looked up. "I don't want to know any of this."

Marjorie reached for his hand but was several inches short of reaching him due to the chair in between them. "I'm sorry you have to hear about this, Ed, especially since he wasn't that good of a kisser to begin with."

"Truly. Keep it to yourself."

She sighed. "All right, so I kissed him back, but once I discovered how bad he was at it, I told him I couldn't go out with him again. Well, we went out that second time, but that was because Sizzler was closing. This is just so embarrassing. I wish Susan wouldn't have told you."

"She didn't."

"Because I like you, Ed." Marjorie smiled. "And not just because you're Santa."

Ed flipped what remained of his sandwich over in his hands. If he added more peanut butter, then he would need more jelly. Otherwise, it would be too dry, and he didn't like dry sandwiches. But more jelly would make the sandwich sloppy, and he didn't enjoy them that way either. Maybe the sandwich was perfect the way it was.

Marjorie forced a chuckle. "I don't want you to think I'm weird and go out with all the guys in the mall. I don't. I've only gone out with Raleigh."

Ed kept his head down. "It doesn't matter. I don't care what you do."

She inhaled deeply, closed her eyes, and held her breath for a moment. When her eyes popped open, she forced a quick expel of air. "Okay, fine. There was also the manager from Specs in the City, but that was to get a great deal on sunglasses. That's all."

Ed shook his head but avoided making eye contact. Maybe he could switch up his type of jelly. He liked grape, but there were other flavors out there. Strawberry and raspberry, for example. Perhaps he could even use marmalade. Would that even go with peanut butter? He'd never heard of anyone doing that.

"Oh," Marjorie said, "I almost forgot about that guy at Death on the Vine."

Ed looked at her now.

"Why are you looking at me like that? I didn't go out with him for a discount on wine. He had a Yorkie that I liked."

Ed bit into his sandwich. Through a mouthful, he said, "Just stop."

"But I'm trying to explain."

"I seriously don't care."

Marjorie frowned. "Then why did you ask about Raleigh?"

"I wanted to know what you thought about him."

"Oh."

Ed stared at her while he chewed.

"You mean for real?"

He nodded once.

"So, you weren't asking about me and him?"

"No."

"And Susan didn't tell you?"

"That's what I said."

Marjorie looked down at her hands. "Well, this is embarrassing."

"Tell about me Raleigh."

"He's all right, I guess—when you get to know him. But he's sort of lazy, if I had to be honest."

"That's what I'm asking."

Marjorie leaned her elbow on the table. "Raleigh's always looking for a way to get out of work and make an extra dollar while doing it."

"Ever hear of him doing anything underhanded?"

"Raleigh's a lot of things, but underhanded isn't how I'd describe any of them. That just sounds so dastardly. He's more inept than anything. That's how I'd describe his kissing, too."

Ed's face flattened.

"Too much information?"

"You said it."

Ed wanted to know what happened between Raleigh and Hurley in the hallway. He was about to ask when Marjorie put her chin back into an open palm.

"Remember when I sat on Santa's lap?" She winked.

Ed shoved his sandwich into his mouth.

"I never got to tell you what I really wanted for Christmas."

He continued to chew.

"You can't chew that forever."

"You're right." Ed swallowed then stood.

"Where are you going?"

He collected his items from the neighboring chair. "Time to go."

"But you're still on break."

Ed grabbed the doorknob. "Christmas waits for no man." With that, he yanked open the door and headed toward the men's room.

Chapter 19

Ed roamed the hallway dressed as Santa Claus. He only had a few minutes left before he was due back at center court, so his pace was quick. He wanted to find Raleigh Dunham. If he couldn't talk with him now, it would have to wait until tomorrow. Raleigh's shift ended before Ed's day on the Santa throne.

"Run, Rudolph, Run," played overhead, urging him onward.

While Ed hunted for the maintenance man, parents moved out of his way and tugged their children close to their sides. The kids openly gawked at him. Grown shoppers pivoted from his path and gaped as he hurried by.

As he passed by the window of a vacant unit, Ed caught his reflection. A hulking Santa stalked forward, arms swinging wide and legs churning as if he were about to break into a run.

Ed slowed and glanced back. In his wake was a swath of concerned families. A mixture of fear and confusion was evident on their faces.

He raised a hand. "Sorry, folks. There's a mutiny with the elves. I need to straighten it out before Christmas."

This brought a smile to several of them before he turned away.

Now, Ed had a new worry—was he losing his marbles? The old Ed—the feared bookkeeper—

wouldn't have bothered with how a bunch of citizens felt. Oh, he might have been concerned about being caught in the wrong place at the wrong time, but just as often, he wanted them to notice him.

Citizens made the best alibis. But they didn't have to like him for that. It might even be more effective if they didn't like him.

Ed was lost in thought when he heard, "Walking around without your handler, I see."

Eileen Webster sidled up next to him. "Saw you stalking around like you were about to kill someone. Thought I should come see what was going on."

"Hey, Eileen. I've only got a few minutes before I'm needed back at center court."

"Why the rush? The party doesn't start without you."

She was right, and a new thought bothered Ed. He was starting to assimilate into normal culture. While with the Dawgs, he answered to no man. His time was his own—he came and went as he saw fit. In prison, he had to be at certain places at a specific time. That's how life behind bars was—there was no choice.

In his first two assignments, the marshals had given him autonomy. He ran a business and went where he liked when he liked. But the last two assignments were actual jobs. His time was no longer his own. He was a member of the working class—a clock puncher.

"Take your time," Eileen said. "Enjoy the walk. What's Susan going to do anyway? Cancel

Christmas because you're late getting back?"

Again, Eileen was right, but Ed liked Susan. As far as bosses go, she'd been a good one. Now, he was putting her feelings above his own. What was happening to him?

Eileen glanced up and down the hallway. "Where were you going in such a hurry?"

"I was looking for Raleigh."

"What do you want with that slacker?"

"Hurley gave him an earful and took his keys."

Eileen's eyes narrowed. "John took his keys, too?"

"That's what it looked like from where I was sitting."

She looked away. "No kidding. It all makes sense now."

"What does?"

"Huh?"

"What makes sense?"

"Nothing." Eileen pointed. "Raleigh is at the end of the mall, sitting on a bench, sulking."

"Why?"

"Who knows? I asked him, but he wasn't having any of it." Eileen patted Ed's arm. "I need to run. There's some stuff I need to take care of."

***

Ed found Raleigh slouched on a wrought-iron park bench. His chin touched his chest while one hand rested on his belly. The other clutched a large cup from Get Your Gulp On.

"How's it going?" Ed asked.

The maintenance man didn't bother looking at him. Instead, Raleigh stared off into the distance and lifted the drink to his mouth. His lips wrapped around the straw, and he sucked. A rattle came from within the empty cup. Defeated, he dropped his hand. "That's how it's going."

"What happened with you and Hurley?"

Raleigh's gaze lowered to the floor. "You saw that?"

"Yeah."

"From your chair, huh? You probably get a pretty good view of a lot of things sitting there."

"Not bad. Did he fire you?"

Raleigh's smirked. "No. What gave you that idea?"

Ed moved so he could see the maintenance man's face. "Hurley took your keys, and you're sitting down here like the world has ended. Simple math says two and two make four."

"You got it all wrong." Raleigh's brow furrowed, and he looked away from Ed. "He didn't fire me."

"But he took your keys."

Raleigh lifted the cup to his lips and noisily slurped air. Frustrated, he waggled the cup. "Yeah, he took them. Then he put me on probation."

"Probation for what?"

He pointed the empty cup at Ed. "Who made you a junior detective?"

Ed scowled, but Raleigh didn't seem to notice.

The effect was mostly lost behind the beard. Ed stepped forward to tower over the smaller man. "Let's try this again."

Raleigh raised his hands in surrender. "All right, all right. I was taking a nap."

"Where'd you do that?"

"In one of the vacants." Raleigh squirmed on the bench and pushed further away from Ed. "Quit looking at me like that."

Ed stepped back and relaxed slightly.

Raleigh lifted the cup to his lips, thought better of it, and dropped it back to his lap. "My father used to dress up every year as Santa. You're bringing back some bad memories."

A woman with several small girls walked by. As they did, the children waved at Ed. He smiled and returned the gesture.

The maintenance man snickered. "You suck at being Santa."

Ed moved forward again.

Raleigh's hand rose in a protective manner. "Take it easy. For cryin' out loud, this is what I'm talking about. Sheesh. What did you want to know?"

Ed tried to appear less menacing—not so much for Raleigh's benefit, but for any families that might be walking by. He lingered on that thought. Was he doing it so it wouldn't look suspicious or so it wouldn't ruin a child's image of Santa? If it was the first, then that was business as usual. If it was the latter, then he needed his head examined.

Ed's eyes narrowed. "You were telling me

about getting caught taking a nap."

"Yeah, whatever. Haven't you ever gotten tired? And haven't you ever thought that it would be great just to lay down for a minute? That's what I did. Now, Hurley's treating it like a federal offense."

"Is that the first time you've done it?"

Raleigh looked away.

"He caught you before."

"Yeah. So? He gave me a warning for it, too. But I only do it on my own time, I swear. Lunches and the occasional break."

"If you were doing it on your own time—"

Raleigh's head bobbled from side to side. "Maybe I overslept once or twice."

"But why take your keys?"

"Hurley said if I couldn't get into the vacants, then I wouldn't be tempted to catch a little shut-eye."

Ed crossed his arms. "Is that so? It seems like a maintenance man—"

Raleigh interrupted by lifting a single finger. "Building engineer."

"What?"

"Technically, my title is building engineer."

Ed stared at him until Raleigh shifted his position on the bench once more.

"I guess it doesn't matter," Raleigh said. "Maintenance man is fine."

"Are you sure?"

Raleigh considered the empty cup he still held. "Yeah. Maintenance man will work."

"As I was saying, it seems like a maintenance

man would need keys to the empty suites."

"I do," Raleigh said. "Or I did. Nobody has rented anything in a while."

Ed glanced back to consider a nearby vacant suite.

Raleigh continued. "It's like the owners aren't even trying anymore. Maybe Hurley is right. If I need to go into a unit, I can go to him for the keys. If they don't care, why should I?"

Ed's gaze returned to Raleigh. "Hurley has all the keys to the vacancies now?"

"He has all of mine."

"And Eileen's, too," Ed said.

Raleigh twisted his lips. "I didn't know that. In that case, yeah, he probably has them all."

"What about a master key?" Ed asked. "Is there one of those anywhere?"

Raleigh absently lifted the cup to his lips and sucked on the straw. It gurgled in emptiness. Frustrated, Raleigh put it on the ground. When he leaned back onto the bench, Raleigh stared at the big man. "What was your question?"

"Master key? Would you happen to know where one is?"

"Why do you care so much about getting into the vacants?"

"Because it feels like Hurley doesn't want anyone going into them. Why is that?"

The maintenance man stood and cocked his head. "That's a good question."

"About that master key?"

A sly grin spread across Raleigh's face. "What kind of building engineer would I be without a backup plan?”

***

Ed was almost back to center court when Chet Malone stepped out of Pet Shop Bays and blocked his path.

“Look who it is,” Chet said. “The interloper.”

“*Chet.*”

“Don’t Chet me.”

Several shoppers with children noticed Ed. With smiles on their faces, they moved toward him. As usual, the kids seemed excited.

Ed looked into the pet store but didn’t see Marjorie anywhere. “What were you doing in there?”

“Wouldn’t you like to know?”

“Not really. I shouldn’t have asked.”

Ed tried to step around Chet, but the smaller man moved and blocked his path again.

“Be careful, Chet. Remember what happened last time.”

“I’m not touching you.”

Now, the folks who stood in line at center court took notice of the confrontation. Susan lingered near the camera-mounted tripod. When she noticed the turning heads, she followed their gaze. Her eyes widened, and she yelled, “Santa!”

Unfortunately, all that did was bring more attention to what was occurring in front of the pet store.

Chet asked, “Where do you think you’re going

in such a hurry?"

Ed pointed toward center court. "To take my rightful place."

"That's my throne." Chet tapped his chest. "*Mine.*"

"Not anymore."

Chet's face reddened. "You stole it from me."

"I didn't steal anything."

Several mall patrons closed in around them. One of them even had a cell phone out to record the moment. Several children waved at Ed. He waved back.

"I say you stole it." Chet stepped closer to the big man. "Like a common thief."

"If it could be taken that easy, was it really yours?"

Chet balled his fists.

"Relax, Chet. There's a lot of witnesses around."

"You think I'm worried about them?" He motioned toward those watching. "Let them witness the fall of the interloper."

Ed held up a defensive hand. "Chet, I'm warning you."

"You're warning me? That's rich. I'm warning you! You caught me by surprise last time. It won't happen again."

"If we fight here, then neither of us will be Santa." Ed tapped his temple. "Think about it."

"I have." Chet brought his fists up into the guard position. "Let's do this."

Ed brought up both hands now and patted the air in a calming manner. "I'm serious, Chet.

I don't want to hurt you."

"Big talk from a two-bit Santa." Chet swung wildly.

The nearby crowd sucked in a collective breath of awe.

Ed, however, simply twisted and lifted his nearest shoulder. Chet's fist bounced off it.

"Watch out, Santa!" a little girl screamed.

A nearby boy hollered, "Get 'em, Santa!"

Chet hollered in anger before swinging again. This time his haymaker thudded onto Ed's elbow. The older man fired two more quick punches that landed ineffectually against Ed's bent arm.

"You're out of your league, Chet. Go back to where—"

But Ed never got to finish his wisecrack because Chet kicked him in the shin. It wasn't the worst pain Ed had ever felt, but it surprised him. He jumped back, dropped his guard, and hopped on a single leg. Chet moved forward and fired several more punches. A couple missed, but one struck Ed right across the chin.

It wasn't enough to render much damage, but it did embarrass Ed. He punched back immediately and caught Chet squarely in the forehead. The smaller man collapsed to the ground.

Several children cheered, but one mother yelled, "Someone call the police! Santa killed that old man." That led to an argument of several shoppers about who was indeed at fault for the fight.

Susan arrived then and twisted Ed away from the crowd.

"What were you thinking?" she whispered. She grabbed his upper arms.

"I was defending myself."

Susan studied the unmoving Chet. "Is he dead?"

"I hope not."

"Why did he attack you?"

"Because I'm Santa."

Her gaze returned to him. "I was afraid this might happen." Susan's fingers slipped into his beard.

"What are you doing?" he asked.

"Your beard is twisted."

Chet's punch, Ed thought. It hit him across the chin. If someone in the crowd videotaped his exposed face, then that was it. They could upload it to some social media platform, and the Satan's Dawgs would find him from there. That's how he was discovered in Costa Buena, California.

"Better," Susan said as she patted his shoulders.

"Did anyone see my face?"

She smiled. "It's so sweet that you're worried about that. No, the beard only got turned a little. Don't worry, though. No children will be traumatized. Well, except maybe seeing Santa in a fight, but since you won, they might have a Chuck Norris version of Santa in their heads now."

Eileen Webster ran down the hall. A massive

set of keys jangled on her duty belt. "Stop fighting! Stop fighting!"

Ed, Susan, and the crowd turned toward her.

Realizing that there no was no longer a fight in progress, Eileen slowed. She addressed the crowd now. "Nothing to see here, folks. Go about your shopping."

"Santa will be back in just a minute," Susan added. She pointed toward center court. "The line starts over there."

Several young boys tugged on their parents' hands to be first in line.

Eileen approached the still prone Chet. "Anyone check to make sure he's okay?"

Both Ed and Susan shook their heads.

The security officer kicked Chet's foot, and the man moaned before stirring.

"He'll be fine," she said. "What set it off?"

"He jumped me," Ed said. "Demanded the suit."

"Shh," Susan said. "People might hear you."

Eileen shook her head. "The way you say it makes it sound like it's got magical powers."

Ed pointed at Chet. "I think it does for him."

Eileen hooked her thumbs into her duty belt. "We should call the cops."

"I think one of the shoppers already did," Susan said. "But what about Hurley?"

"What about him?" Eileen and Ed asked in unison.

"Aren't you going to notify him, Lee?"

Eileen shrugged. "I probably should."

Ed eyed the security officer.

"Although, I haven't seen him around. Have either of you?"

"Not since he took Raleigh's keys." Ed's gaze dropped to Eileen's duty belt. "Looks like you got yours back."

Her grin was sheepish. "Guess he had a second thoughts. He left them in my office."

"That was nice of him," Susan said.

"I thought so."

"Are you going to handcuff Chet?" Ed asked.

Eileen muttered, "Right," and reached for her cuffs, but they weren't on her duty belt. Her face flushed. "I must have left them in the security office when I ran down here."

Marjorie appeared in the doorway with three Pomeranians at the end of the leash. Each dog seemed freshly washed and trimmed. Marjorie's eyes widened as she saw Chet lying on the ground. "What happened?"

"Chet ambushed Santa," Susan said. "It didn't go well."

Marjorie moved closer to Ed. "Are you okay, Santa?"

The little dogs strained against their leashes as they tried to get closer to Chet.

"I'm fine," Ed said. "What was Chet doing in your store?"

Marjorie motioned toward the dogs. "He was getting his boys trimmed for the holiday. Meet Dasher, Prancer, and Blitzen."

The dogs licked the fallen man's face.

Susan frowned. "I told you. Chet really got into the whole Santa thing."

Chapter 20

"Were you scared?" The little boy named Jeremy stared at Santa.

"No," Ed said. "But let's talk about you. What do you want for Christmas?"

"I would have been scared."

"Why's that?"

Jeremy looked down. "I don't like to fight."

Ed cocked his head. "Do you get into fights a lot?"

"No, but there will be mean kids at school. I know it."

"You haven't even started school, and you're already worried about the mean kids?"

"They're waiting for me. I know it."

Ed looked up at the boy's mother and father. They stood side by side and watched with eager attentiveness. "What do your parents say?"

"They won't let me home school. That's what I want to do. There are no bullies at home."

"How about some boxing lessons?"

The boy's face creased. "I'm four."

"It's never too young to start."

"Nuh-uh."

From behind the camera, Susan Roskam lifted her thumb. "We're good," she said. She moved to the opening of the velvet ropes.

"How about a punching bag?" Ed asked Jeremy. "You can hit it whenever you want."

The boy shook his head.

"All right, just tell me what you want, and let's wrap this up. There are eight—" Ed looked up in time to see another family join the line. "Ten kids behind you now. Make it quick."

"I want a shark."

This surprised Ed. No other child had requested such a thing. A couple of kids had requested a puppy. One wanted a kitten. The one girl wanted a magical flying pony that fetched, but none had asked for a fish, let alone a shark.

Ed bent toward Jeremy. "Any specific kind?"

"A big one." The boy spread his arms wide. "Like this."

"Where are you going to keep it?"

"In my room." Jeremy nodded as if he were imagining the shark hanging with him in his bedroom. "I'll feed it and everything."

"What are you going to feed it?"

"The mean kids."

"The mean kids who you've never met?"

Jeremy nodded.

"All right, buddy. Get after it." Ed lifted the boy from his knee and announced, "He wants a shark."

The boy didn't seem thrilled by Ed's announcement, however. Instead, Jeremy seemed resigned to a future of bullying. His shoulders slumped forward, and he trundled back to his parents. He had the same shuffle an accountant develops for his daily walk to the office.

Two uniformed cops approached Susan then—Lobdell and Duffy. Ed relaxed in his throne and watched them. The two officers spoke briefly with her then Lobdell moved toward him. Duffy stayed behind to talk further with Susan.

"So, this is where you work?" the cop asked. He glanced around, taking in the massive Christmas tree and the line of waiting families. "Still hard to imagine you as a San-tey Claus."

"Did you arrest Chet?"

Lobdell's gaze returned to Ed. "He's been detained until we finish our witness interviews."

"One woman got the whole thing on video."

"Did you get her name? Because she didn't come forward."

Ed sighed. "Figures."

"Chet says you hit him because you were jealous that he was talking to the owner of the pet boutique."

"Is that so? And what did she say?"

"She said she didn't see anything, but she made it seem like there might be a thing between you two. So, maybe what Chet is saying is true."

"There's not a thing."

"You sure? She likes you."

"I'm sure there's nothing there—yeah. Chet swung at me because I took his job."

Lobdell pressed his lips tightly together. "Him, I could see in the suit. He looks like a San-tey Claus."

Officer Duffy came over then. "She saw the

whole thing." He thumbed back toward Susan. "Said the old guy punched this one—" He thumbed toward Ed now. "—several times until he got himself knocked out."

Lobdell crossed his arms. "Huh."

"What's wrong?" Ed asked.

"I don't know. You're made up like Kris Kringle, but it all feels wrong." Lobdell looked back at the line of families. "And the kids like you?"

"They seem to."

"Willful disillusionment, huh?"

Ed didn't know about that, so he let it slide. "Would you do me a favor?"

Lobdell frowned. "Now, you want a favor from us. You think we're friends or something?"

"It's about the Santa suit you guys took from my apartment."

"You want it back?" Lobdell leaned in. "Finally going to admit it's yours?"

"When you get Chet down to the station, ask him to try it on."

Lobdell's brow furrowed. "You don't think."

"I don't know what I'm thinking. I'm just asking for a favor."

The older officer rubbed his face. "We'd have to ask Detective Novak about it."

Duffy chimed in. "He'd probably say okay."

"But we'd still have to ask," Lobdell said.

Ed nodded. "I'd appreciate it if you would."

Lobdell looked toward his partner. "Anything else?"

The younger officer eyed Ed. "If it wouldn't be

too much trouble."

Ed knew it wasn't because of him—it was the suit—but a cop had never wanted a picture taken with him. He enjoyed the irony of it. "Why not?"

Duffy moved to the side of him. "Come on, Lobdell. Get in on this. For the wives."

The older officer grunted. "If you tell anyone else about this."

Ed said, "Who am I going to tell? I work with kids."

The three of them smiled at Susan. She stepped behind the camera. "Ready," she said. "All together. Merry Christmas."

The two officers called out, "Merry Christmas!"

Ed sat silently and thought about the choices that led him to this moment.

***

Ed walked down the corridor to the breakroom. He had a couple of things left to do after the mall closed, so this long day wasn't quite over. But the first thing he had to do was get out of the tomato suit.

He put his hand on the breakroom's door and paused. The light to the mall office was on. He hadn't seen John Hurley since he'd given Raleigh an earful and taken his keys away.

Ed stepped over to the mall office and looked through the small window. No one seemed to be inside, but he couldn't see into Hurley's office.

A handwritten note was affixed to the door—
Went home for the day. It was written in block
letters.

He tried the knob, and the door opened. Ed
stepped inside and listened. There wasn't any
noise.

Ed coughed loudly in case someone stepped
out and greeted him. No one did.

He moved quickly toward the mall manager's
office. The chair behind the desk sat empty. The
light to the room was still on. Papers were
stacked orderly next to the computer.

Ed didn't know much about computers.
When he was with the club, most activities
requiring a computer were left to the prospects
or the girls affiliated with them. He knew
enough basic skills to get around on one,
though. He thought about calling up an Internet
browser and going to
thefbiisabunchofdirtyrats.com. However, he
was afraid of a couple of things.

First, what if there was a way that Hurley
could tell he visited that site? Then the mall
manager might discover who he really was.
Second, what if the mob could track him back
to this computer? He decided discretion was
needed at this moment.

He did, however, move the computer's mouse,
which lit up the screen. An email program was
the first thing that came to light. Out of
curiosity, he scanned the various emails. Most
of them seemed like tedious functions related to
mall operations. Requests for lease renewals.

Janitorial complaints. Accounting questions. One email caught his eye, though.

Scheduled Date for Mall Closure—January 15th.

Ed clicked on the email, and a window popped open. He skimmed it then went back through it a second time. Ed hit the print button, and a printer in another room started up. He closed the email window and left Hurley's office to find the printer.

***

Ed finished changing out of the Santa uniform just before Susan entered.

"Perfect timing," she said.

"Any earlier, and you would have caught me without my pants."

"Then it wouldn't have been perfect."

She picked up the folded Santa suit that was stacked on the table and stuffed it into its carrying bag. Then she carried it to its usual corner of the room.

"One more day," Susan said.

"Christmas Eve," Ed agreed.

"It'll be a short one. The mall closes at six."

Ed opened his locker, reached in for his jacket, but paused. His eyes returned to the bag containing the Santa suit. She only laundered the suit when something dirtied it, or it got too smelly. This suit was doing fine and would last one more day. Then she could put it away for the year.

"How many suits do you have?" Ed asked.

"Just two. This one and its back-up."

"I meant different sizes."

Susan nodded. "Gotcha. Same deal. I got a number of them like that—two apiece. My mom used to run this business, then I took it over from her. She'd been here almost thirty years."

"That's a lot of Santa suits."

"A few."

Ed pulled his jacket from the locker. "Where do you keep the suits when it's not Christmas season?"

"The mall lets me keep them in one of the storage units in the basement. It's part of our deal."

"How often do you go down to them?"

"Not very often. Once the season starts, of course, to pull everything out and schlep it up to center court. Then at the end to drag it back down."

"And that's it?"

"Not much other reason to go there."

Ed pointed to the suit in the bag. "Where's the sister suit?"

"In the trunk of my car. I keep it there for emergencies so I can get it to you quickly. Who knows when we might need to swap it out?"

"Mind if we go down to the basement and take a look around?"

Susan shrugged. "What for?"

"I'll tell you when we get there."

"I knew you were going to say that."

Susan led Ed down a set of stairs then through a twisting maze of corridors until they ended up in a long room of storage units. Aging fluorescent lights bathed the basement in a sickly, yellow glow. A hum from the lights and other mechanical equipment drowned out the silence Ed had expected.

"The tenants can rent these," she said.

Most of the plywood lockers sat open and unused. Ed poked his head inside one where only a wooden chair remained on its side. The storage unit appeared to be about ten feet squared. The walls did not go to the ceiling, leaving a gap between neighboring units. When he stepped back into the hallway, he said, "Doesn't seem to be much demand for them."

"A sign of the times." Susan tapped on locker seventeen. "This is mine." After slipping a key into the lock, it popped open.

Ed followed her in. "How do you fit the Christmas tree in here? It's huge. There's no way it could fit in here."

"Oh, the tree isn't mine. That belongs to the mall. They store it elsewhere. The throne, stanchions, and other stuff, that's mine. This is plenty of room for what I need." Susan walked over to a shelf lined with various bags. "Here are the other suits." She patted one of them. "There's one suit in each of these."

Ed walked over and squeezed the nearest bag. It felt full. Was it worth it to pull each bag down and peer inside? He thought so and was about to do so when something caught his eye. Next to the bag he just squeezed was a footprint with a complex pattern on the shelf. The Santa boots he wore were smooth soled. The print couldn't have come from one of them. On a lower shelf were several pairs of black boots. Ed picked a pair up. They also had smooth soles. He put the boots back and returned to the bags.

Susan said, "There's one suit in each, in case you're wondering."

Ed stepped back to get a better view to make sure he was counting them all. "How many suits do you have?"

"Eight. A main suit and back-up for each size." Susan's gaze drifted over the bags.

Ed's suit was in the breakroom, and his back-up was in Susan's car. That meant there should be six bags on the shelving unit.

"Wait a minute," Susan said. "There's only five." She spun around to take in the rest of the storage unit. "One of them is missing. Where did it go?"

"I have an idea," Ed said.

She faced him. "You think the mall robber used it?"

"Maybe."

"But I have the only key to this storage unit. It's my lock."

Ed looked toward the ceiling and studied the gap. A man could easily slip through there. The most challenging part would be getting up to that height to do it.

Briefly, he studied the footprint next to the bag before uttering, "Wait here."

"Where are you going?"

He went to the neighboring unit on the left, but it was empty. Nothing was left behind to aid in someone's climb. He jumped for the gap, but it was out of reach.

Ed went to the unit on the right. It was also barren inside.

When he returned to the hall again, Susan stepped out from her storage unit. "What are you doing?"

"Looking for a ladder."

"The maintenance room is upstairs."

"Yeah," Ed said, but he didn't think whoever did this would go upstairs and ask for that item. He returned to the first storage unit he had peered into when they entered the basement. The wooden chair lay on its side. When he righted it, he noticed another footprint on the edge of the seat. Ed carried the chair into the hallway.

"Someone stood on this," he said

Susan stopped to examine it, but Ed didn't hang around to discuss it. He moved into the next unit. There he found a wooden crate. It also had a footprint on one side. "Bingo," Ed muttered.

"What's bingo?" Susan called from the hallway.

Ed stepped out of the storage unit carrying the crate. As he passed Susan, he snatched up the chair.

"Hey, I was looking at that."

"Come with me."

Susan followed him. "You think that's how they did it?"

"We'll find out."

When they returned to the neighboring storage unit on the right, Ed set the chair down, then stacked the wooden crate on top of the seat. He quickly ascended it.

"Be careful," Susan said. "We've got one more day to go."

"Thanks for your concern."

"You know what I mean."

The gap was now easily within reach. Ed heaved himself up and into Susan's storage unit. When he fell to the ground, Susan walked around to join him.

"Okay," she said. "Now, we know how they got in. But the door was locked. How did they get out? They didn't have the chair and crate in here."

Ed walked her over to the shelving unit where the Santa suits were stacked. He pointed to the footprint he saw earlier. Then he noticed another on the shelf below it and above it.

"Son of a gun," Susan muttered. "In one side and out the other."

"Not the hardest heist ever." Ed was sure this one wouldn't have caused either Parker or Dortmunder any problems.

Susan put her hands on her hips. "Then whoever it was went back and moved the chair and crate so it wouldn't look like someone broke in.”

Ed nodded. “Just in case someone noticed.”

“Pretty clever. And you think this was the suit they found in your apartment?”

“I’m guessing. If not, the smart thing to do would have been to return it.”

“Do you think it could be the convenience store robber?”

Ed shook his head. “I doubt it.”

“Why not?”

“There’s something else going on there.”

“Like what?”

Ed shrugged a single shoulder. “I don’t know yet, but when I figure it out, I’ll let you know. For now, though, I want to find Hurley.”

Susan’s eyes widened. “You think he stole the suit?”

“I think there was a fight earlier in the mall, and he didn’t make an appearance.”

“Yeah, that was weird.” Susan made a skeptical face. “But why should we care? It’s nice when he’s not around.”

“A fight involving Santa Claus on the day before Christmas Eve should bring the mall manager out.”

“You’re probably right.”

They stepped out of the storage unit, and Susan locked it. “I need to report the missing suit to the police.”

“Hold off on doing so.”

Her eyes widened.

“Just until the time is right.”

“I don’t get you playing detective.”

"Trust me," Ed said. "Please."

They headed toward the exit.

"Now, you've got me worried," Susan said.

"There's nothing to be worried about."

"But what if we can't find Hurley?"

Ed led the way up the basement stairs. "Then go home and act natural."

"Is that what you'll do?"

"Sure."

"Why don't I believe you?"

At the top of the landing, Ed held open the door. "I've got something else I need to do tonight."

"Care to share?"

"Probably better if I didn't."

Susan's face flattened. "These plans better not have anything to do with Marjorie."

Ed smiled. "I don't want to be part of any small-town gossip."

Chapter 21

The address wasn't too far for Ed to walk. Even though the night was cold, he pulled his stocking cap down a bit tighter, hunched his shoulders a little higher, and jammed his hands into his pockets. A shopping bag dangled around his left wrist.

He thought about grabbing a cab, but there weren't many of them to be had in Utopia. He would have had to call a dispatch service, but his phone was still in his apartment. So, he'd have had to borrow a phone and then request the ride, which meant at least two people who might remember where he was going.

Utopia wasn't a small town, it was a small city. Someone had told him it contained roughly forty thousand people. Even so, getting around was easy if one were patient and willing to walk. And Ed had nothing but time. The only thing he had to look forward to tonight was reading *The Hot Rock*, but that could wait.

Ed entered an older neighborhood filled with decaying homes, broken fences, and snow-covered sidewalks. In almost every window, a large screen television fluttered with images.

It took only a few minutes for Ed to find the home he sought. It was a small affair that had seen better days. Unlike its neighbors, however, the porch light wasn't on, and no television played in the window.

Out front, a mid-eighties Monte Carlo sat on concrete blocks. Behind it sat a dented Subaru Baja. A yellowing streetlight flickered.

Ed approached the house and knocked. A moment later, a woman opened the door. Behind her, playing on the floor, was the boy named Asher.

"Can I help you?" the woman asked.

"Is Rodney here?"

Susan had shown him the photograph request form for Asher. The boy's father had filled it out. That's how Ed had learned of the address and the man's name—Rodney Clellan.

Suspicion clouded the woman's eyes. "How do you know my husband?"

"We're old friends."

She shook her head. "I know all his friends."

"Okay, you caught me. I'm Santa."

The woman stepped back to appraise Ed. "Of course, you are."

"I am."

"All right then." She glanced over her shoulder. When she looked back, she whispered, "What does Asher want for Christmas?"

"He doesn't want anything."

"Wrong," the mother said. "He wanted a football. Santa said so." She started to push the door closed. "It's time you go."

Ed removed the bag from his wrist and handed it to her. "I picked this up before I left the mall."

The woman's gaze softened as she peered inside the sack. "How did you know?"

"Asher didn't want anything for Christmas, so I suggested the football for him."

Her eyes registered confusion.

Ed said, "He told me how hard it's been for you guys."

"It's fine." She looked back toward her son. "We'll be fine."

"What's your name?"

"Mary."

"Mary, I know what Rodney has been doing."

She looked away. "I don't know what you're talking about."

"Of course, you do. He needs to stop before something bad happens."

Ed heard a shuffle of feet behind him and turned to see Rodney Clellan walking up the sidewalk. His face was flushed from exertion, and his hair was matted to his forehead from sweat. Cupped in the crook of his arm was a brown grocery bag. Even from just a glimpse, Ed knew what the red fabric inside it was from. He'd seen it almost daily for the past month.

"Who are you?" Rodney asked.

"This is Santa," Mary said. "From the mall."

"He doesn't look like a Santa."

She lifted the bag and opened it to reveal the football. "He brought Asher a gift."

Rodney's lip curled. "We don't need your handouts, man. Take your charity elsewhere."

"I didn't come for Asher," Ed said.

"Yeah? What did you come for?"

"I came for you."

Rodney's hand moved toward the bulge in his jacket pocket. "You a cop or something?"

"Take it easy," Ed said. "I only want to talk."

"Rodney," Mary said, "Asher is on the other side of the door."

"What's he doing there?"

"Waiting for you to come home."

Rodney moved his hand away from his pocket. He then pushed the brown paper bag toward Mary. "Take this and go inside. There's some goodies in there."

She nodded in understanding, took the sack, and closed the door.

When it was just the two men, Rodney's face hardened. "Quit with the act, tough guy. What do you want?"

"If I came to make your life difficult, we wouldn't be talking. It would just be happening."

Rodney blinked. "What kind of Santa are you?"

"The kind who makes house calls."

"But..." Rodney cocked his head. "Isn't that what Santa does?"

Ed waved a hand. "Where'd you get your suit?"

"What suit?"

"The Santa suit you handed Mary."

Rodney's eyes narrowed further. "You sure you're not a cop?"

"I'm not a cop. I just need to know about the suit."

"I got it at a thrift shop earlier in the year. Paid cash for it." Rodney's gaze drifted toward the house. "I thought it would be a neat surprise for Asher at Christmas time. You know, surprise him and all. The kid loves the holiday. Then things got rough around here and seeing it in the closet one day gave me an idea."

"To make some house calls of your own."

Rodney rubbed a hand over his mouth. "What are you doing here, man? I don't even know you."

"I'm here to tell you that you've been made."

"How so? Nobody's seen my face. The cops haven't trailed me once. Seems I've got this thing whipped for at least a couple more days. When the holiday stops, I'll stop." He smiled. "Until next Christmas, that is."

Ed pointed at the tattoo on Rodney's wrist. "They've got a photo of it." Ed didn't know if that was true, but he didn't want to say that Nathan the clerk saw it. Doing so might put Rodney on a path of revenge.

Rodney placed his hand over the tattoo. "The phoenix? So what? I haven't been arrested since I got it. Therefore, the cops know nothing about it. It's not like there's a national tattoo registry."

"Sooner or later," Ed said, "they'll find someone who says they know you and that tattoo. That's how the cops are. When they find that link, you're done for. Take it from someone who knows." Ed showed him the inky ball of fire on the back of his right hand.

"You got a criminal record? But you're a

Santa."

Ed shrugged. "It didn't come up during my interview."

"How could it not?" Rodney studied the inky bird on his wrist. "You think maybe I should get it removed?"

"I think you should quit while you're ahead."

Rodney's features tightened. "Are you kidding me? My whole life, I've struggled for a job and some money. Now, I've finally found something I'm good at, and you want me to stop? Why should I listen to what you say? I don't even know you, man."

"I've been you," Ed said. "Trying to find the right path but walking the wrong one."

"What I know is I've finally got some money in my pocket. Things are looking up for us. We paid our rent. Got a Christmas turkey. There's no way I'm stopping. You can't be for real."

"The path you're on only leads one way, and that's to prison."

"What is it with you and paths?" Rodney cocked his head. "Are you like the Ghost of Christmas Future or something?"

"I'm just a guy trying to be a better man. You want to continue doing this, then so be it. I can't make you change. But there's a kid in there that loves you so much he didn't want anything for Christmas."

"Santa said— *you* said he wanted a football. You even brought him one."

"I brought it because he said you've been struggling. That's why he said he didn't want anything.”

Rodney looked toward the closed door. “I never said anything to him.”

“Whether you did or didn’t, he heard it.”

“Now what? You think telling me this will make me stop? Turn over a new leaf, maybe?”

“No,” Ed said. “I’m telling you if you pull another job, I’ll call the cops.”

The words felt foreign in Ed’s mouth. Worse, they felt wrong. He’d been forced to rat out his club, but that was to protect his grandmother. Since then, he’d solved a couple of crimes because of the implications law enforcement made about his involvement. Had he not been thrown into the mix, Ed would have acted according to one of his favorite mantras—live and let live.

Now, here he was sticking his nose into another man’s business—another man’s life— when there wasn’t any real reason except maybe the kid who sat on his knee and talked about his struggling dad.

Parker and Dortmunder wouldn’t do something like this. But McGee would. Always like the good guy more, Sorrell Babin had said. Maybe this is what he meant.

Rodney glanced around before whispering, “You’ll call the cops? What’s stopping me from shooting you right here and now?”

“Nothing. So, pull it out.”

“What? Are you crazy?”

“Shoot me.” Ed put his finger in the middle of his forehead. “Put it right here and pull the trigger.”

Rodney glanced around again. “I’m not going to do that. This is my house, and the cops will come. I’ll be done for sure.”

“That’s right. They will come. Guaranteed.”

“There’s something messed up in your head.”

“No,” Ed said, “I see things clearer than I did before. Stop what you’re doing and be a hero to that kid.”

“Or what?”

“Or go to prison. It’s your choice.”

“It’s not a good choice.”

Ed smiled. “I said the same thing not too long ago.”

“Now, you’re taking it out on me?”

“That’s how life is.” Ed turned to leave.

“Wait.”

He stopped.

Rodney looked down at his hands. “I guess I should be grateful.”

“Let’s not make this a Hallmark moment.”

“It’s not that.” Rodney touched the tattoo on his wrist. “You gave me a heads up about this. I still don’t understand why you would do such a thing.”

“I don’t know.”

“Ah, come on, man. You got to have a reason.”

“Call it a Christmas miracle.”

Rodney shook his head. “You don’t seem to be the type to get into the holiday spirit.”

“Let’s say it’s growing on me.” Ed headed down the sidewalk.

***

The doorbell chimed as Ed entered the convenience store. Another annoying rap song played from speakers hidden somewhere above.

Nathan the clerk stood in the middle of the store dancing and singing to the song. "My truck, your truck, pressin' our luck." He swung his arms across his body. "Down in the holler for a twelve-point buck."

When he noticed Ed, Nathan straightened. The music overhead continued without him.

"Yo, Big Time," Nathan said. "Here for another *el burrito grande*?" He snapped his fingers. "The hunger satisfier."

"I'm in the mood for something different tonight."

Ed headed toward the cooler, and Nathan followed along.

"Fighting the habit, huh? I get that. Burritos three nights in a row is enough for any man. Starts to mess with the ol' digestive tract. Want a recommendation?"

"I think I'm good."

"Stay away from the egg salad sandwiches."

Ed looked back over his shoulder.

"For real, though. I don't trust the expiration dates on them. And they never taste right even when they're brand new."

Ed turned his attention to the cooler. The options for dinner were limited. There were frozen burritos, frozen pizza, and frozen turnovers. For those semi-fresh items, there

210

were sandwiches, wraps, and salads. Among those selections, the remaining items looked picked over. Only one or two of each item remained.

He really should go to the grocery store. The selection was better, but it was inconvenient. It took him a cab ride to get there, then a cab ride home. He could probably take the bus but taking that ride with a couple of bags of groceries bothered him. Not that many people didn't do it, but he used to be the bookkeeper for the Satan's Dawgs. He had a reputation to uphold. Certain things just bothered him.

But what would a trip matter? Christmas was here in a couple of days, and this gig would be up. Marshal Goodspeed would return with some new location and cover. Ed wondered if she would let him stay a few days or not. Not because it was the holiday—that didn't mean anything to him. He wondered if it might mean something to her.

Ed opened the cooler, made his selection, and headed for the front of the store.

"No way," Nathan said with a laugh. "I'm gonna have to start calling you Mister Predictable."

Did he care what this clerk thought of him? Were his actions becoming too predictable? Did his food choice make him a bad person?

The big man tossed the Big Time burrito onto the counter. Then he went back and grabbed a red Gatorade and a bag of barbecue chips just to switch things up. He wasn't predictable.

Nathan rang up the items and announced the total.

Ed handed him several bills then eyed the police flyer hanging behind the register.

"Yo," the clerk said, "did you hear? He robbed a joint over on Elm Street earlier tonight."

"Is that so?"

"Got away clean, too." Nathan shook his head. "I don't think anything is gonna stop him."

"You'd be surprised."

"You think he's gonna have some change of heart or something and not pull another job?"

Ed twisted his lips. "Who knows?"

Nathan laughed. "Dude! Get real. That stuff only happens in those hokey movies my mom watches."

***

When the door to his apartment opened, the cat chirped and sprinted across the room.

"Hey now," Ed said and gently pushed Travis away from his leg. "We had a deal."

The tom attempted another rub, but Ed shook his leg.

"Go on."

He was in the kitchen before he realized it. The apartment remained as clean as he'd left it in the morning. That's not to say Ed was a clean freak—he wasn't. He just liked things orderly. Time spent in a small box courtesy of the state penal system had taught him to put things where they belonged.

The cat, on the other hand, liked chaos. Travis seemed to delight in knocking any unsecured item to the floor.

Had there been a breakthrough? Had the tom finally realized he needed to behave by a different set of rules to coexist peacefully?

Travis attempted a third rub against Ed's leg, and this time the big man let him. Ed even bent over to pet the tom. However, as soon as he reached down, the cat bolted into the other room.

"Finicky guy," Ed muttered.

He set his bag from the convenience store on the counter then refilled the cat's food and water bowls. When he was done, he put the burrito in the microwave and started the time.

He checked the clock—it was almost ten. He had a couple of hours to kill before his next errand.

Maybe he could grab a quick nap, although that might just make him more tired for what he had to do next. Ed crossed his arms, lowered his chin to his chest, and closed his eyes.

When the microwave dinged, there was a small crash in the other room. Ed stepped around to see what the commotion was.

Travis had knocked over a lamp.

"That's how it's going to be, huh?"

The cat darted underneath the bed.

Chapter 22

The Superior Mall's parking lot was almost deserted. Only two cars remained in the lot. A blue BMW was in the area designated for employee parking, while a red Toyota was near the loading dock.

Ed crossed the lot with his hands jammed into his pockets. The stocking cap pulled down over his ears did little to protect against the cold. As he neared the entrance, a rusted pick-up pulled up to the front.

After the engine of the yellow truck quieted, it continued to knock and ping for a few moments. The driver's door squeaked as it opened, and Raleigh Dunham climbed out.

"Got your master key?" Ed asked.

"Of course," Raleigh said, "but I wasn't sure if you were putting me on."

"It's midnight. Why else would we be here?"

The maintenance man looked around. "I don't know. Maybe you get insomnia and wanted a friend to hang out with."

"Do I look like I need a friend?"

Raleigh shrugged. "Everybody needs friends."

Ed pointed at the BMW parked in the far lot. "Whose car is that?"

Raleigh squinted. "That's Hurley's."

"So, he's still here." Ed and Susan couldn't find him before leaving for the night.

"And that one?" Ed pointed toward the red Toyota near the loading dock.

"That's—"

An unmarked patrol car pulled up then.

"It's the cops," Raleigh said. "Act natural." He turned away from the approaching cop car and began whistling, "Take Me Out to the Ball Game."

Detective Stewart Novak climbed out of the passenger side. "This better be good, Belmont."

Raleigh whispered, "He knows your name."

"Detective Novak," Ed said, "meet Raleigh Dunham, the mall's maintenance man."

"Building engineer," Raleigh corrected.

The detective nodded. "We've met." To Ed, Novak said, "So, why do you have me out past my bedtime, Belmont?"

Raleigh lifted his hands in surrender. "I didn't have anything to do with this, Officer. He's the one responsible. He made me come tonight."

Both Novak and Ed stared at the maintenance man.

"What?" Raleigh continued. "Ed told me to be here, and I did as he said. I mean, look at him. He's intimidating. I can't get in trouble for being intimidated. Can I?"

The detective faced Ed. "Are you sure this guy is with you?"

"He is, and we're about to crack your case."

"We already cracked the case, Belmont. With your help, no less. You tipped us to have that Chet Malone character try on that Santa suit. Fit him like a glove. The guy didn't have an alibi for the night of the robbery either."

Ed shook his head. "Chet didn't rob the fundraiser."

Novak seemed taken aback. "What? But you were the one who told us about him."

"Don't get me wrong, it's the suit he wore when he was Santa, but he didn't rob the mall."

The detective looked to Raleigh. "Are you following any of this?"

Raleigh shrugged. "I haven't followed anything since I got here."

Novak eyed Ed. "I don't know what you're up to, Belmont, but you got me here, so make it quick. You're affecting my beauty sleep."

Ed motioned toward Raleigh. "Get us in."

The maintenance man moved toward the entrance but paused with his key at the lock. "He's making me open this door. You see this, right?"

Ed frowned.

"Fine, fine," the maintenance man mumbled. "Nobody cares if I get in trouble." He unlocked the door and pushed it open. "It's always the little guy who gets squashed in these types of things."

As they walked into the mall, Ed said, "The problem with the fundraising heist—"

"Where are we going?" Novak interrupted.

"It's up ahead. As I was saying, the problem with the fundraising heist wasn't how they got in—"

"It wasn't?" Raleigh interrupted.

"No," Novak said. "We already know this."

The maintenance man furrowed his brow. "Well, I don't. How'd they get in?"

As the three men turned a corner, Ed said, "There are businesses, corridors, and a basement that someone could hide in. And since Hurley cut the security back from twenty-four hours, it's possible anyone could stay here after the mall closed."

"Ah," Raleigh said. "Makes sense."

"Right," Ed said. "Which means the problem is getting out."

Raleigh stopped and pointed back to the doors they had just walked through. "Getting out is easy. All exits have crash bars. Just push them, and the door will open. They are locked from the outside but can't be permanently locked. It's a fire code thing."

Ed waved them onward. "I should have said the problem was getting the jugs of money out. There were too many to get out in one night."

"Not if it was a crew," Novak said.

"But it wasn't," Ed said. "It was one guy."

Now it was Novak's turn to stop. He crossed his arms. "One guy?"

"That's what I'm saying."

"If one person pulled that heist, how would they get those jugs of money out? The witnesses said there must have been at least seventy-five. A crew pulled the job, Belmont. It had to be."

Raleigh raised a hand as if he were in a classroom. "One person could get them out in a single night if they used a hand truck."

Novak pointed to the maintenance man. "The

mall should have one of those."

"We do, but it's broken. Been that way for weeks."

"You can't go out and buy a new one?"

The maintenance man shook his head. "It's crazy what's going on around here with the budget cuts. We can't buy nothing new because of Hurley the cheapskate. We have to fix everything with bubblegum and a band-aid."

"So, Belmont, your lone heist man brought his own hand truck."

"He didn't," Ed said. He started walking away.

"How do you know?" the detective asked.

"Call it an educated guess."

"What makes you so educated about this?"

He pulled *The Hot Rock* from his coat pocket and handed it to Novak.

"A book?"

"Not just any. It's about a heist."

"You're a reader?" Raleigh's face squished with incredulity. "Who knew?"

The detective studied the paperback as they walked. "And this somehow allows you to make an educated guess?"

Ed hadn't read enough of the novel yet to know whether it did or not. However, by the way Novak examined the back cover, Ed was reasonably confident the detective hadn't read it either. Due to this, Ed felt safe saying, "Call it inspiration."

"I'm up this late at night because of your inspiration? I'm liking this less and less."

"Have some faith, Detective."

"Now, I'm supposed to have faith, too?" Novak returned the book to Ed. "This whole adventure hinges on your hypothesis that a singular guy carried those jugs out by hand."

"Did he?" Ed asked.

"Did he what?"

"Carry them out?"

"Now, you're screwing with me. Your buddy here just said the hand truck is broken."

"Think about it," Ed said. "Those jugs would be heavy. All those coins and bills would add up to a lot of weight."

"The bills don't add much," Raleigh said. "It's the coins."

Ed glared at the maintenance man.

"I'm just saying."

Novak grunted. "We thought about this, Belmont. That's why there had to be more than one suspect. It had to be a team that took down this job. Your faith and inspiration aren't going to carry the weight on this one."

Ed shook his head. "I'm telling you it was one guy."

"How do you figure one guy with no hand truck? There's no way he carried them out of the mall."

"I agree."

The detective cocked his head. "So what? You think this guy drove a vehicle into the mall?"

"No," Ed said. He hadn't thought about that, and maybe it could have occurred, but he had a pretty good idea of what did happen. They stopped at the front of the mall office hallway.

"John Hurley's office is down that way."

"I know," Novak said. "I've been there. And that's where they stored the jugs after the event. Tell me something I don't know."

"My shop is over there, too," Raleigh said.

Novak frowned. "How'd the jugs get to and from the event?"

Raleigh laughed now. "Oh, man. You should have seen it. What a nightmare. All the stores had to bring them down before the event. There were some unhappy employees waddling down carrying them jugs."

"And none of the stores had a hand truck for their employees to use?" Novak asked.

Raleigh cocked his head. "I guess there were some. Yeah, now that I think about it. A couple of the bigger ones had them. So, I could be right! The robber could have used one."

"No hand truck was used," Ed said.

"How do you know?" Novak asked. "Never mind. I know. Inspiration and faith. Right?" The detective's gaze returned to Raleigh. "So, this nightmare with the jugs? What was that about?"

"That was getting them to the mall office. One at a time. By myself. Man, I was wiped out by the end of that."

"You didn't have any help?"

"Nope. Just me. Hurley kept after me, though. Like a drill sergeant. He was timing me, too. Really pushing me to keep going. Like it was an Olympic event or something."

"Hurley didn't bother to help?" Ed asked.

Raleigh shook his head. "Not once. I thought

he'd pitch in a little, being so close to Christmas and all, but he said to look at this as a challenge. To see how fast I could move the jugs."

This revelation seemed to intrigue the detective. "And how long did it take you?"

"About three hours," Raleigh said. "By the time I was done, I was ready to go home and take a hot shower. I could barely lift my arms. My legs felt like jelly. But I did it."

"One guy," Novak said. "Three hours. Hurley couldn't have been incapacitated for that long."

Ed nodded. "I agree, and we'll get back to that." He motioned in a circle. "Take a look around, Detective. From where we stand, there are four vacant units."

Novak's eyes traveled the same path that Ed's hand had taken. "What about them?"

"If you were going to hide seventy-five jugs in plain sight, where would you put them?"

The detective put his hands on his hips. "Any of them would work, wouldn't they?"

"Yeah," Ed said. "Why don't we try this one." He walked over to the vacant suite between Kitchen Stitches and Hair Today Gone Tomorrow. Its windows were blacked out. Ed pulled on the door, and it opened.

"Did you unlock that before I got here?" Novak asked.

Ed shook his head. "Not me."

"It should be locked," Raleigh said.

The detective removed his pistol and stepped into the unit.

As Ed and Raleigh followed behind, the door closed behind them. Plastic jugs filled with coins and bills were placed at the front of the suite, but what was behind them was of more interest.

Laying on the floor was John Hurley. His hands were cuffed, and his legs were zip-tied. A gag was stuffed in his mouth and secured to his head. His eyes widened when he saw the three men. The rag muffled his voice.

"Holy cow!" Raleigh said. "Someone kidnapped Hurley!"

Novak stepped forward and pulled out a set of keys. He bent next to the mall manager and inserted a key into the handcuffs. "Hold on, Mr. Hurley. You can tell me all about it in just a minute."

The door to the suite opened, and Eileen Webster stepped inside. She wore a blue sweatshirt and faded jeans. Her eyes widened when she saw the three men. "Oh no," she muttered.

Eileen bolted back through the door.

Novak pointed at the door. "Go after her, Belmont!"

Ed stepped back. "I'm Santa, man. Not the law."

The detective jumped to his feet. "I'll remember that." He raced into the hallway.

***

Several minutes later, Detective Novak returned with Eileen Webster. He held her by the elbow as her hands were now cuffed behind her back. When Novak noticed that John Hurley still lay on the ground with the rag stuffed in his mouth, he eyed Ed. "You could have helped the man up."

"We didn't want to disturb the crime scene."

"That's right," Raleigh added. "In case you needed to get photographs or something."

Novak positioned Eileen away from the door. Then he attended to Hurley. In a moment, the mall manager was seated upright with the rag removed from his mouth, and his hands set free.

"Tell me what happened," Novak said to Hurley.

The mall manager massaged his wrists as his eyes flicked from the detective to Ed. When his gaze settled on Eileen, he said, "I discovered what she was up to and—"

"Liar!" Eileen shouted.

Novak lifted a hand. "Ma'am, I advised you of your rights. If you continue—"

"But he's lying!"

"Ma'am," Novak said. "Let him finish. You'll get your opportunity."

Hurley stood but continued to rub his wrists. "I found her here, in this unit, with these jugs of money, but she overpowered me."

Novak glanced back at the security officer. "She overpowered you?"

Hurley nodded. "That's right."

The detective faced the mall manager. "I don't see it."

"I guess I'm not a very good fighter."

Ed leaned toward Novak. "Eileen can fight. I've seen it. She flipped a teenager like she had some training."

Eileen glowered at him. "Thanks for the help, Ed."

Novak studied Eileen for a moment then turned to the mall manager. "You think she dressed up in a Santa costume then attacked you?"

Hurley nodded. "Why not?"

"But you said it was a man." Novak jerked his head toward Ed. "We even asked about Belmont. You didn't think it was him, but you said it was a man."

The mall manager appeared sheepish. "I must have been wrong."

"Uh-huh. What about the voice?"

"Maybe she lowered it," Hurley quickly said. "Can you get her to do it now?"

As Novak turned toward her, Eileen muttered, "Not a chance."

"There's your answer," Novak said.

"It makes sense." Hurley continued rubbing his wrists.

"What makes sense?" the detective asked.

Hurley stepped toward the side. "Eileen. She had access to the basement where she stole a costume. Then she put it on and robbed me."

"A lot of people have access to that basement," Eileen said. "You have access. Raleigh has access. So do Ed and Susan. Most of the retailers in the mall do, too."

"What basement?" Novak asked.

"The mall has a basement," Ed said. "There are storage units down there. That's where the Santa set-up is stored along with the replacement costumes."

Hurley continued. "But Eileen had to have taken it because she's here. Right? She overpowered me after I found her here with the fundraiser's money. Then afterward, she took the Santa suit to Ed's apartment to frame him for the crime."

"I didn't do that," Eileen protested. "It wasn't me! I don't even know where he lives."

Novak faced Ed. "Has anyone checked this storage unit?"

"We did."

"And?"

Ed nodded. "Someone broke into the unit and stole a costume."

"And you didn't report this?"

"We just learned about it earlier today. Susan was waiting to report it until I talked with you."

Novak's lips twisted, and he crossed his arms. "Why wait?"

"Because there are footprints on the shelves that the thief climbed to get out."

When Novak looked at Eileen, she smiled.

"What's so funny?" the detective asked.

"They aren't mine. I was never there."

Hurley pointed. "She's lying."

Eileen swung a foot and kicked one of the jugs. The mall manager jumped back.

"I admit I tied him up," Eileen said. "I'll even

admit I was stealing these jugs from him, but not the fundraiser. Check my car. There are a few in there now, and I've got some at my house already. I promise you this—John Hurley stole them first."

The mall manager shook his head. "This is a baseless accusation. You got no proof."

Novak rubbed his chin and his gaze swept between the mall manager and the security officer.

Ed said, "Ask about the keys."

The detective eyed him. "What keys?"

"Hurley took her keys to all the vacant units. Then he took Raleigh's, too."

"That's true." Raleigh nodded. "He did."

"That's because I couldn't trust you to do your job," Hurley said.

"He wanted to limit everyone's access to the vacant suites," Ed said. "Then I saw Eileen with a big ring of keys later in the afternoon."

"That's after I caught him in here," Eileen said. "I took them back."

"What was he doing in here?" Novak asked.

"Just checking on the jugs, I think."

The detective considered the plastic jars. "How much money do you figure is in each jug? A couple hundred bucks?"

Ed shrugged.

"Two hundred times seventy-five. That's what? How much?" Novak glanced at each person in the small suite.

Ed was much better at counting than multiplication. He furrowed his brow in mock concentration. He didn't want to have the blank stare that Raleigh now did.

"Fifteen thousand," Novak said finally. "That's a lot of money, but is it worth losing your job over?"

"He was already losing his job," Ed said. "The mall is closing."

"What?" Raleigh blurted. "Who says?"

"Sorry, Raleigh. I saw the notice in Hurley's office."

Hurley's face reddened. "You were in my office? That's trespassing." He turned to the detective. "Arrest him."

Novak studied Ed. "Did you break into his office?"

"No. I saw it when he called me in."

"That's impossible," Hurley said. "I never printed out those letters. The only way you would have seen them—" He stopped talking.

The detective moved closer to the mall manager. "So, you were about to lose your job. Maybe you thought the fundraiser's money would come in handy."

"It wasn't me." Hurley pointed to the security officer. "It was her. She did it."

"I'll admit to what I did," Eileen said. "Believe me when I say this, he stole the money first. I was only stealing it from him."

"I think there's one thing left for us to do," Ed said.

"What's that?"

"Check Hurley's shoes against the footprints in the storage unit. If they match—"

The mall manager sprinted for the door, but Ed stuck out his foot. Hurley stumbled into the hallway before sprawling onto the floor.

Detective Novak hurried out and grabbed him. Once he lifted Hurley to his feet, he said, "I think we're going to need some additional officers."

Chapter 23

Ed pulled on his Santa's pants just before Susan Roskam burst into the breakroom.

She wore a square box wrapped in Christmas paper. Affixed to the top of her head was a large, red bow. "Is it true?"

"I'm still changing."

"It's not like I haven't seen that sort of thing before."

"Not with me."

She looked away. "Is this better?"

"I've already got my pants on."

Susan spun around. "Then what's your problem? Is it true? Did the cops really arrest Hurley and Eileen last night?"

"Got 'em both for theft."

"No way!" She grabbed a chair and dropped heavily into it. The back of the box she wore loudly crumpled. "So, Raleigh is in charge right now?"

"For a few days at least."

Susan shook her head. "Until they get a replacement manager hired. That could take weeks."

Ed picked up the Santa jacket and slipped it over his shoulders. "There's something I've got to tell you."

She lifted her head. "What now? Is someone else going to get arrested?"

"The mall is closing."

"Yeah. It closes early every Christmas Eve. I already told you that."

Ed continued to button his jacket. "That's not what I'm talking about. I saw a letter on Hurley's computer."

"You broke into his office?"

"That's not the point."

"You could get us in trouble. And then where would we be? Without a Santa is where." She pointed out of the room. "Did you think about those kids?"

"Listen to me."

She shook her head. "No, you listen to me. Those kids depend on you. You're Santa. In their world, that's a huge deal. There may be no more significant responsibility than being Santa. Do you understand?

Ed inhaled deeply. "The mall is closing next month."

Susan blinked several times before saying, "You're serious."

"Hurley was supposed to send out letters to all the retailers, but he failed to do it. He kept the news hidden."

Susan's blinking increased. "Why would he do that?"

"I don't know, but that's one of the reasons he was letting people go left and right. It's also why he wasn't repairing things."

"What am I going to do?"

Susan leaned forward. However, the box she wore pushed up under her chin and against her throat. She tugged it away, but that didn't give her enough room. Susan angrily jerked at it then beat her fists against the sides until the box folded enough for her to lean comfortably forward. She no longer looked like an unopened Christmas present. She looked like one that had been sent through the mail.

"Easter is right around the corner," she muttered, "and then it'll be Christmas again. Where will we go next year?"

Ed slipped the thick black belt around his waist. "You'll figure something out."

She flopped back into her chair and covered her face with her hands. "This is horrible news."

"We've got one day left, Suzy. Deal with it after that."

Susan shook her head but didn't remove her hands from her face. "It's not even worth it. Years of work down the drain."

"Don't talk that way."

She spread her fingers to look at him. "I'm serious. Go home, Ed."

"We can't do that."

"No one will care," Susan whispered.

"I'll care." Ed pointed out of the room toward center court. "Those kids who are coming today will care. We need to go out and give them a good memory before this mall closes forever."

Ed didn't really care whether or not he went back out there. He liked Susan and didn't want her to feel defeated right before Christmas. She was too nice to have to experience that on her favorite holiday.

A small, sad smile crossed her face. "I guess the holiday spirit has finally arrived."

***

The little girl named Savannah stared at Ed with intensity. "I want world peace."

"For Christmas?"

"Uh-huh." Savannah was six years old with a wrinkled brow and the piercing eyes of a parole officer. "My mother said that I could have anything, and that's what I want."

From behind the camera-mounted tripod, Susan Roskam lifted a hand. "Good." She didn't sound very enthusiastic.

Ed nodded at Susan then eyed the kid again. "That's all you want—world peace?"

"Uh-huh."

"I'm not sure that will fit in my sleigh."

Savannah patted his arm. "It doesn't need to fit in anything, Santa. I know that."

Ed glanced at the girl's mother. She wore an olive-drab coat previously worn by a soldier. On it were buttons of various sizes that promoted love, harmony, anarchy, and voting for Kerry/Edwards. She flashed Ed a peace sign.

He looked back to the girl on his knee. "Christmas is tomorrow."

"I know."

"I'm not sure I can get world peace done by then."

"Why not?" Savannah shifted her position so she could study Ed closer. "Why can't you get it done?"

Ed sighed and looked away. There were only two hours left in his shift as Santa, and he was looking forward to this assignment being over. He'd heard about the rings of hell but didn't know anything except they corresponded with levels of hardship. Ed was sure that children must be one of them.

Savannah patted his arm again. "Why, Santa?"

"Because there are a lot of moving parts to world peace. Lots of people to talk to and issues to work out. Smarter people than me haven't been able to pull it off."

"There's no one smarter than you."

Ed shrugged. "It's hard."

"But you're Santa. You can do anything."

"Still. These things take time."

"Next year then?"

Ed wasn't going to be here next year, so he didn't see the harm in telling the kid he could deliver world peace. "Yeah. Why not? So, what do you want this year?"

"Nothing."

"Are you sure? Not even a Barbie or football?"

Savannah slipped from his knee. "Nope. I'm good." She turned and raised her hands in victory. "Santa is bringing world peace!"

The crowd cheered. Savannah's mother clapped approvingly.

From behind the camera, Susan shook her head in dismay.

***

Ed handed Susan the folded Santa suit. "For the last time."

"Yeah," she said dejectedly. "Maybe forever."

He watched silently as she stuffed it into its bag. Susan paused mid-shove and looked back. "Who stole the suit from my storage locker?"

"Hurley did. We matched his shoe to the footprint."

"And he broke into your apartment how?"

"He took the key from my pants while they were in the storage locker. He must have seen my address on my driver's license, too."

Susan nodded. "If he would have gotten the right-sized pants, things might have turned out differently."

"But since you keep the backup pair in your car, he took what was available. I got lucky."

"That's one way to look at it. And he put the suit and jar in your apartment for what reason?"

"A diversion," Ed said. "He stole the money then hit himself to make it look like he was robbed. Since Hurley had access to a suit via the basement, all he had to do was figure out someone to blame."

"Why not blame the convenience store robber?"

"There was a chance that guy could get caught," Ed said. "What Hurley needed to do was cast an additional aspersion. I was the most natural since I was sitting in center court all day long."

"Do you think he did it because you guys didn't get along?"

Ed shrugged, then nodded. "Probably, and why not? It would be a bonus if the cops arrested me. Regardless, as long as they focused on me, it took any interest away from him."

"It seems like a lot of risk for not much gain."

"It was all cash," Ed said. "No one put checks into those jars. It was all coins and bills. The cops still have to count everything they recovered in those jars, but Detective Novak estimated fifteen thousand."

"That's a nice severance package."

"Not nice enough. He's going to get a few years for it."

"What are you going to do now?" Susan asked.

"I don't know." It was an honest answer.

***

Ed walked through the hallways of the Superior Mall for the final time. "It's Beginning to Look a Lot Like Christmas" played overhead. He didn't feel melancholic about the moment. Ed rarely felt that type of emotion.

Marjorie Lewis trotted up next to him. She wore a sweater and blue jeans. She was dressed almost normally today. "You're the talk of the mall today."

"How so?"

"You got Hurley and Eileen arrested. That's hard not to talk about."

Ed shook his head. "I didn't do anything."

"Whatever. What are you doing tonight?"

"Same thing I do every night."

"But it's Christmas Eve."

Ed shrugged. "For me, it's Thursday."

"Do you want to know what I'm doing?"

"No."

She playfully slugged his arm. "You're so funny. I'm waiting for Santa, of course."

"It's not happening, Marjorie. I've told you. I've got a girlfriend."

"I didn't say I was waiting for you."

"But you said Santa."

"Yeah," Marjorie said. "The real Santa. I go to my parents' house, and we make cookies for Santa. Then in the morning, we open the presents that he delivered."

Ed stopped walking. He wanted to ask if she knew that Santa wasn't real, but it seemed a subject that could lead to unexpected consequences. If she didn't know, well then, she was a loon, and he didn't need to be in this conversation any further. If she did know, she would continue talking with him, and that wasn't ideal.

She stared at him, waiting for him to ask his question.

"Sounds like fun," Ed said and continued walking.

Marjorie hurried back to his side. "You can come over if you want. We drink eggnog, sing songs, and play games."

"No."

Her brow furrowed. "Is this the last time I'm going to see you?"

"Probably."

"We're never going out, are we?"

"The Sizzler closed," Ed said. "I think that was the sign."

"Yeah," Marjorie muttered. "Darn it."

She turned and headed back toward her shop.

Chapter 24

Ed awoke to a knocking. He shuffled across the apartment in his shorts and t-shirt. He opened the door to find Sorrell Babin standing there with a plastic bag in his hand.

"Merry Christmas, my friend."

Inside the sack were three novels—Lawrence Block's *Burglars Can't Be Choosers*, Elmore Leonard's *Get Shorty*, and Janet Evanovich's *One for the Money*.

Ed smiled. "Thank you."

Travis wandered out of the apartment to rub on Sorrell's leg. The older man leaned down to pet the tom.

Ed closed the bag. "Do you want to come inside? I can put on a pot of coffee."

The older man straightened then covered his heart with a hand. "None for me, thank you. I am on my way to spend the day with some friends. What about you? What are you doing?"

"You're looking at it."

Sorrell's face registered sadness. "But it's Christmas. Would you like to come with me? I am sure there will be enough food."

"No," Ed said. "You go on. I'll catch up with you tomorrow."

Reluctantly, Sorrell shook Ed's extended hand. When the older man wandered down the hallway, Ed closed the door.

After making breakfast, Ed sat on the edge of his bed. His apartment was clean, and the dishes were washed. He thought about reading *The Hot Rock*—maybe he could even finish it today—but a wave of loneliness washed over him. This emotion surprised Ed as he didn't usually feel these sorts of things.

He'd been alone often in his life and been okay with it. Was it the recent experience as Santa Claus and all the talking with children that put him into this state? Whatever it was, he had an overwhelming urge to call someone.

Ed reached under his pillow and pulled out his cell phone. There were only two people he wanted to talk with at this moment—Daphne Winterbourne and his grandmother.

He flipped open the phone and stared at the illuminated screen. Calling either of them was against the rules and could put them both in danger. Ed loved his grandmother enough not to do that, and he never wanted to bring any harm to Daphne.

A sigh escaped his lips. Ed snapped the phone closed.

Ed bolted awake when there was another knock at the door. *The Hot Rock* slipped from his chest and fell to the floor. Travis ran into the kitchen.

"Hold on," he muttered.

The knocking was persistent.

"I said hold on." He yanked open the door.

Marshal Goodspeed stood there with a look of irritation on her face. "Are you ready?"

Ed eyed her. "Ready for what?"

"To go. It's time we move you."

"But it's Christmas."

Goodspeed put one foot into his apartment and craned her neck. "Oh, I didn't know you had a party going on in here. You want me to come back?"

"Yeah," Ed sarcastically said. "I want you to come back."

"Too bad. My Christmas is ruined, so yours might as well be, too. Pack your stuff. You're moving."

"But nothing bad has happened. I don't need to move."

Goodspeed entered his apartment now. "Where's that good boy of yours?" Travis came out of hiding. "There he is."

"Where are we going?"

"Don't worry about it. You'll like it."

"I didn't like this place."

The marshal scooped up the cat. "You did fine. More than fine, you thrived."

"How do you figure? I barely kept my job—"

"But you kept it."

"I only met a few friends—"

Goodspeed nuzzled Travis. "But you met some."

"I almost got arrested by the cops—"

"But you didn't. You complain a lot."

Ed stared at her for a moment.

"Anything else?" Goodspeed asked.

"Do I get a say in where I'm going?"

"No."

Ed threw his hands in the air. "I want a say the next time."

"There better not be a next time."

"At least give me a hint where I'm going."

"It's not Minnesota."

"Thank God."

She set Travis on the floor. "Now, pack your bags. We got some driving to do."

The marshal left his apartment.

Ed stood in the middle of the living room. "So, this is Christmas."

Travis trilled and ran to him. The tom turned in a couple of circles before rubbing against his leg.

Ed pushed the cat away. "That's enough of that. Let's not get carried away."

Beau Smith
returns in...

Cozy Up
to Danger

ABOUT THE AUTHOR

Besides writing the Cozy Up Series, Colin Conway is the author of the 509 Crime Stories, a series of novels set in Eastern Washington with revolving lead characters. They are standalone tales and can be read in any order.

Colin is also the co-author of the Charlie-316 series. The first book in the series, *Charlie-316*, is a political/crime thriller and has been described as "riveting and compulsively readable," "the real deal," and "the ultimate ride-along."

He served in the U.S. Army and later was an officer of the Spokane Police Department. He has owned a laundromat, invested in a bar, and run a karate school. Besides writing crime fiction, he is a commercial real estate broker.

Colin lives with his beautiful girlfriend, three wonderful children, and a codependent Vizsla that rules their world.

Learn more at colinconway.com.